Preface

A newspaper article on Ostend, my previous novel, triggered a deep emotional crisis and a need for clarification. Two Euro Candles wasn't planned. Not exactly. I didn't come to the shores of the North Sea searching for miracles. I came because the air is heavy with salt, because the sea slaps the promenade with the same indifferent rhythm that's always felt like home, and because I needed somewhere to sit quietly with myself without anyone noticing I was falling apart.

It's not a theology of candles or a study of saints. It's not a self-help manual or an attempt to unpick trauma with neat psychological bows. It's a collection of moments—unvarnished, sometimes awkward, often absurd. It is what happens when a runaway boy grows into a runaway man who finds himself lighting €2 candles in a historic church, whispering silent confessions to stone statues, and hearing whispers back.

You will read about burnt coffee and lost hoodies, seagulls that refuse to leave, and prayers that sound like last-ditch text messages sent at 3 a.m. You will meet Saint Thérèse of Lisieux, not as a plaster-cast relic, but as a sharp-witted, irreverent companion who has no patience for self-pity yet sits quietly with the world's pain.

These pages hold pieces of my life: childhood violence wrapped in suburban normality, generational trauma that seeps unspoken through flipped dinner tables, grief that sticks to your ribs long after everyone else has moved on, and the fragile joys that make all of it bearable.

If this book has a purpose, it is not to instruct or inspire, though you may find both within it. Its purpose is simpler: to hold a mirror to the quiet parts of ourselves we rarely acknowledge. To name the shadows we carry into churches, laundromats, cafés, and empty bedrooms. To remind us that we are all cracked vessels carrying prayers we are too scared to speak aloud.

I don't know if miracles exist in the way people hope they do. But I know that lighting a €2 candle for someone else, whispering their name into the flickering silence, feels like a miracle in itself. I know that grief, when witnessed with honesty, can become a form of prayer. And I know that sometimes, the saints speak back—not with thunder or visions, but with a quiet, irreverent nudge towards your

memoir
Book 2026

TWO EURO CANDLES

A Memoir of Faith, Trauma
and Quiet Miracles

MAXSENSE MAXIMUS

Content Advisory – MA15+

This book contains mature content including trauma, emotional distress, references to suicide, and spiritually provocative reflections. It is recommended for readers aged 15 and over.

Two Euro Candles is a work of literary memoir. While all efforts have been made to approach the subject matter with sensitivity and care, some readers may find the material confronting.

Reader discretion is advised.

Printed on-demand at various locations.

For more information: www.maxsensemaximus.com

Book design by Maxsense Maximus

Cover design by Maxsense Maximus

ISBN - Paperback: 978-0-6488470-6-9

ISBN - Ebook : 978-0-6488470-7-6

First Edition: July 2025

Dedication

To L.N.L.L.

Also by Maxsense Maximus:

Ostend

Table Of Contents

TABLE OF CONTENTS

TABLE OF CONTENTS

TWO EURO CANDLES

own trueness.

If you find something of yourself here—some grief, some laughter, some stubborn hope—then let it be a candle lit for your own journey.

Welcome to Two Euro Candles.

TWO EURO CANDLES

Chapter 1

Coffee That Tastes Like Regret

The coffee was burnt.

That was the first sign.

It came in a paper cup that disintegrated slightly at the seam, leaking warmth onto my thumb before I could find a table. I stirred it anyway—wooden stick, weak swirl—and took a sip that made my eyes water.

Welcome to Ostend.

I sat by the window of a small café that had no name on the door—just the words Warme Drank in faded blue. It was mid-morning and already cold, though the locals didn't seem to notice. A man rode past on a bicycle with a baguette under one arm and no helmet. A woman walked a terrier wearing a puffer jacket fancier than mine. Both had some proudness attached to their motion.

I'd arrived late the night before. The rental car at Amsterdam Airport had been delayed just long enough to make me think about bailing on the first leg of the trip. I didn't, of course. Ostend is my favourite. And my weakness. I told myself I needed a break. A reset. An adventure. The fresh air of the North Sea. A holiday, technically. Though I'd packed like I was fleeing something. I am a runaway boy. A runaway man.

I'd booked a modest Airbnb near the centre. My holiday rental hostess was kind to me. She accepted a late check-in. The flat smelled faintly of tidewater and lemon cleaner—the kind that never quite covers the scent it's meant to replace. There was a double bed and a bookshelf stacked with Dutch romance novels and cookbooks from the '80s. The Wi-Fi was barely legal. But the electric heaters worked, and that felt like a small mercy.

That morning, I woke early. Didn't check the time—just knew. My body carries a kind of grief-clock these days. It rings soft but deep. I served myself a glass of tap water, left it undrunk—it was too cold. Got dressed in yesterday's clothes and wandered until I found the café.

Now here I was, sipping regret in a cup, watching people pass by who had no idea I'd come here to fall apart politely.

The café played music from a pair of mini speakers near the ceiling—something vaguely French, heartbreak lyrics and dub beats. The singer had a smoked voice similar to

Serge Gainsbourg. The smell of the cigarette Gitanes was missing—like the grace and lyrical pleasure of his song Histoire de Melody Nelson or Cargo Culte.

My phone is my writing companion, my lightweight typewriter. It had travelled across countries with me and was ready to capture miracles—if they exist. Google Docs is the recorder of my pilgrimage.

It had been a few weeks since I'd left anything meaningful on the screen. Maybe more. Work reports didn't count. Nor did birthday messages. I hadn't forgotten how to write. Ostend is only once a year. My screen is filled with bullet points waiting for editing.

A woman entered the café. Middle-aged. Not in a romantic way—just in a real way. She wore a coat that looked like it had weathered more winters than most marriages. She ordered in fluent Flemish, her cosmetic face smiled at the barista, and she sat down with a sigh that felt like relief.

I wanted to tell her that. You sighed like relief. Like arrival. Like surrender. But of course, I didn't. I just looked out the window and took another sip. I wish I could sigh like her.

Outside, the wind picked up. A man's hat blew off, and he chased it without any hope. Just instinct.

My coffee was nearly gone. It hadn't improved. But I drank it anyway, because I'm the sort of person who finishes things even when they're not worth finishing. Projects. Conversations. Relationships. You name it.

I am not a quitter. I am always the last man standing. Nothing to be proud of. It's a vulnerability. I don't know how to say "no" or acknowledge—and, most importantly, accept—when things are over. It's my secret disability. My tender weakness.

The woman stood to leave, brushing chocolate croissant crumbs off her lap. She looked at me as she passed and gave the smallest nod. Nothing intimate. Just I see you.

It undid me a little.

Not dramatically. Just enough to let a crack open. A hairline fracture in the armour I wear like politeness. An armour that defines my identity.

I finished the last bitter mouthful. Tossed the cup in the bin near the door and stepped out into the cold, unsure where I was going.

And there it was, just around the corner and without surprise— The Church of Saint Peter and Saint Paul.

Massive. Plain from the outside. Quiet in a way that drew you in without asking. I paced myself to go inside that day. Just stood across the street and looked at it like someone sizing up a stranger they'll eventually fall in love with. I am no stranger, and I am already in love. She, a neo-Gothic beauty, is my Ostend ritual. My reason to be here.

I did go inside. I couldn't resist.

Later that night, back in the Airbnb, I made milky rooibos tea I would dreamily slurp. Sat on the bed. Picked up my phone. Scrolled back through my previous Google Docs entries. My past visits and observations at the church had a tone of spiritual ignorance. My focus at the time was on the folklore and the choreography of the faithful, the pilgrims of the ordinary, the soul-bearers, the parade of contradictions, the saints in progress and the sinners on pause. It's always cinematic, dramatic—pulsed by a touch of sadness and a brush of authenticity.

My journal entry for 11th November 2023 reads:

> *The door groaned behind him, its iron hinges letting out a whine as it shut. Cold, damp air clung to his exposed skin, mixing with the residual warmth of incense and stone. He stood still for a moment inside the narthex, heavy breath rising slightly in the colder air, his chest moving with the effort of quietening whatever noise was trying to claw its way out from inside him.*
>
> *It appeared that the man was built for highways, diesel roars and gear scraps, not sanctuaries and penance. His flip-flops smacked gently against the polished grey floor; the slap oddly obscene in a space made for whispers. The cold hadn't dissuaded him from wearing what he always wore: a sun-bleached Metallica T-shirt that used to fit years ago, stretched now across his belly, the hem curling upward to reveal the pale underside of his oversized gut. His arms hung loose—too long, too tired—like they'd forgotten what to do when not wrapped around a steering wheel.*
>
> *The church's nave unfolded around him like a deep breath. Shadows of blue, green, crimson and gold played on the stone columns, moving slowly across the floor in fractured stained-glass*

light. Above, the neo-Gothic arches soared, disappearing into vaulted heaven. Somewhere, far off, an invisible pigeon cooed. The silence wasn't silent—it was thick with weight: of footsteps past, of unspoken prayers, of guilt hanging in the cold.

He made his way down the left aisle, limping slightly, the left flip-flop dragging more than it should. He didn't look at the altar, didn't scan the pews. His eyes were fixed—dull and red-rimmed—on the far wall. He moved like someone who didn't want to be seen, but didn't care if he was.

There, tucked against the side wall beyond the last row of pews, was a mosaic—a luminous apparition of Mary, pale as milk and etched in white tesserae, her expression unreadable, her arms open as if forever catching the falling. A black steel stand rose before her like an offering platform, holding a sea of candles. A few flames already danced within their glass cups, flickering in the holy draft and quietly welcoming everyone with the same warmth.

He stood there for a long time, the toes of his right foot curling against the edge of his flip-flop, as if gripping the ground might stop whatever was shaking inside him. The cold pressed in from the stone floor and the soft draughts, but he barely noticed. His shoulders were hunched, rounded from years behind the wheel, but today they sagged differently. His inner scaffolding had buckled. His eyes scanned Mary's face, searching for something—recognition, forgiveness, a reprieve.

His hand, cracked and calloused, slid into the front pocket of his jeans. He pulled out a coin—warm from his palm—and slipped it into the slot. The sound it made, dropping into the metal tray, echoed absurdly loud in the stillness. He picked up a candle—white, slim, cheap—and struck a match. The first scratch failed. He tried again. The second caught. His hand shook slightly as he lit the wick. The flame caught, then steadied—small but unwavering.

He didn't kneel. He didn't cross himself. But he stood there, eyes on the flame, lips pressed together, jaw tight. His nostrils flared slightly with each breath, and his bottom lip twitched as if something wanted to speak but couldn't get out. His fingers trembled by his sides.

Outside, Ostend sat under a grey sky, the sea not far, the air biting at four degrees. But in here, beneath the kaleidoscope of sacred light, the man looked as though he might combust from the inside out.

He blinked—twice, slow—and a tear slipped down one cheek. He didn't brush it away. It dried there, carving a line through the stubble and salt.

The scent of the church filled his lungs—old wood, wax and dust warmed by the sun filtered through saints and martyrs. And something older, ancient maybe: the petrichor of stone, the unyielding memory of a building that had seen wars, weddings, death. A smell like contrition, if there were such a thing.

Finally, he shifted. One hand reached out and touched the base of the stand—not to steady himself, but to say something. I was here. I did this. Then he turned, slower than before. Each step was deliberate, his body heavier now, as if the air around him had changed density.

He didn't look back at Mary.

He walked towards the exit, the light behind him painting his silhouette in fractured grey glass. His shoulders, still slumped, didn't rise. There was no redemption yet. Just the dull echo of flip-flops on stone—a man-shaped void trying to carry itself back into the cold world.

After reading my journal entries, my fingers couldn't stay steady on the phone keyboard that night.

Except for our mind, we've got nothing to conquer or challenge. As we live, we carelessly fill our headspace with real stories, self-imagined events, distorted truths, friends and enemies, gods and demons—priceless and costly educations that create endless chaos we're not even aware of. We are lifelong garbage collectors with little power to recycle or process. I am no better.

My ignorance has defined how I've perceived life until now. It has shaped my identity and, sadly, most of my reactive behaviours—the ones that make me dance or try to conduct the orchestra of my emotional headspace. It's hard to become the observer of your own chaos. To let go of unnecessary control in the pursuit of clarity. It's even harder to resist the pull of those reactive behaviours, which instinctively tempt you to jump back onto the dance floor and perform your lifetime misery.

I'm tired of being a poor actor. A lousy dancer. A first-class loser.

I just want to be a witness—not the marching band leader who tries, unsuccessfully, to control, process, correct, or convert the noise of outdated, unhealed emotions, unresolved traumas, and unprocessed personality quirks into a half-decent melody no one but me will ever hear.

I want to stand on the kerbside of my own existence and observe my internal fanfare play out its outdated choreography before it disappears forever around the street corner.

I am looking for silence. A sigh. A gateway to joy. A trampoline back to myself.

Clearing the mind should be as simple as tapping a glass of sparkling water on a tabletop and watching the carbonated bubbles rise, pop, and dissolve into the holy nothing. Straightforward. Instantaneous. Selfishly easy.

Ostend, please take my armour away. I will accept the fragility of my authenticity.

I want to be me.

I desire to be me.

TWO EURO CANDLES

Chapter 2

Speed Prayers And Silent Despair

If there's a queue for miracles, it moves fast.

I started timing them—don't ask me why. Maybe out of boredom, maybe curiosity. The average person spent under three minutes in front of the statue. Some didn't even stay long enough for the candle wax to melt. Light. Flick. Mutter. Exit. Next.

It reminded me of takeaway orders: no eye contact, lots of urgency, no time for extras. These weren't pilgrimages. They were pit stops. Faith on a timer.

There was the bloke who ran in wearing a hi-vis vest, a hard hat and steel-cap boots, still dusty from work. He lit his candle like he was trying to outrun something—maybe a divorce, maybe his debt. He mumbled something under his breath before bolting back out.

A middle-aged woman came next, wearing a designer coat three sizes too big and mascara smudged like war paint. She looked like Cruella de Vil in The Hundred and One Dalmatians. She whispered so softly I couldn't hear the words, but her posture screamed, please. She didn't kneel. She crouched, like someone used to being knocked around.

Then came a young fella dressed like a Bronx hip-hop wolf wannabe. He's maybe twenty, earphones still in. Lit a candle without removing them, lips moving to whatever track was playing. A whispered, "Universe, tap in—your boy manifestin'!" escaped him before he gave Mary a subtle swagger and walked off like he'd just closed a deal.

It was wild. Heartbreaking, actually. The way people pleaded with the divine like they were sending voice memos into the void. So much desire, packed into tight little parcels of time and wax. It felt transactional. But also, raw. Desperate. Human.

I tried to keep my distance—emotionally, I mean. I tried not to dance someone else's emotions. But every now and then, someone would say something that landed right in my chest. One girl—no older than ten—lit a candle, looked up at Mary, and said, "Please make Mum stop crying at night." Then walked away like it was normal.

My mum cried at night and woke up with black eyes. I was that little girl fifty years ago and I didn't know you could pray to make it stop.

I didn't succumb to the emotional rowdiness of my inner marching band. I didn't pick an instrument. I didn't dance. I stayed still. It was a heartfelt and hurtful celebration. Ten-year-old kids have only the power of their prayers to change the world.

What struck me most wasn't how many people believed. It was how few of them actually expected anything to happen. Their prayers sounded like last-ditch texts you send at three o'clock in the morning—just in case someone's still awake.

From where I usually sit, Mary's ceramic display and the candle rack are on my left, and the statue of St Thérèse of Lisieux is on my right. Her face is teasing me. It's hard to say if she's smiling or grinning. I can't stop looking at her. It's like a fixation or an addiction. My mind—which doesn't help—tries to levitate her from her plinth. If I were to succeed, it would be a miracle. My miracle.

I'm not great on Catholic stories and so on, but between Mary and Thérèse, Thérèse is my favourite. She is a writer. After reading her letters, I realised we have something in common. Her little flowers are my "Less is More". Her presence and silence calm me. She makes me experience other dimensions.

If she could talk, what would she say to me? Maybe her silence is her way to communicate. Two ears, one mouth. Is she a listener? Or maybe a professional observer laughing somewhere, watching me fall headfirst into other people's grief and nightmares.

It made me wonder if the miracles people wanted were really the miracles they needed. Or if they just wanted to know someone heard them at all.

The church filled and emptied like a lung.

Breathe in: the young, the old, the lost.

Breathe out: silence, flickering lights, the smell of smoke and shoe polish.

And Mary, still standing, still listening. Still stone.

Thérèse made me curious.

Chapter 3

He Looked Like My Brother

Back in the Coldness of the North Sea

I recognised him by the way he walked. That slouching, uneven rhythm—left foot just a little lazy, right one dragging it forward like it had somewhere better to be. His electrician's back gives him some grief.

He was standing near the jetty, staring out at the sea as if it had betrayed him. A thin, salt-worn jacket, long hair blown across his forehead. And that stance—a quarter-defensive, three-quarters offensive—the same one I hadn't seen in years. Not since I migrated overseas.

I didn't call out. I didn't move. I just stood there and stared like a wimp. A poor observer watching a lion in his primal habitat.

It wasn't him, of course. The man turned slightly, and I saw it—different nose, different eyes. But for a moment, I'd believed it. Felt it in my gut. My heart had gone soft and stupid in my chest, and I hated it for doing so.

I love my brother. His name is Greg.

My younger brother by six years—and a few decades of chaos.

That part is always hard to explain.

He blames me for running away. His fragile mental state is my fault. That's what he says.

I had no choice. It was all about survival. I couldn't stay. I didn't want to stay. It was my right to break down the ugly emotional generational cycle. My kids deserved better. Much better. Even raised on the opposite side of the world, they were—and are—somehow the victims of the downfall of my non-cohesive upbringing.

Trauma is a tricky bastard. It doesn't care about timing. It doesn't care about bloodline. It just arrives, decides where it wants to sit, and dirties the joy of life for us to clean.

Sometimes it chooses the chest. Sometimes it picks the throat.

That day in Ostend, it chose tears. Rivers of them.

I sat down on a cold bench by the promenade and watched the not-Greg walk away. My hands were shaking. Not much. Just enough to remember I was still full of things I hadn't said.

Or haven't healed.

We hadn't fought, exactly. Just grown apart the way people do when pride, pain and stubbornness are louder than love.

Every now and then, I message him just to reassure myself of his welfare.

Today, I did. It was short: "I am in Belgium."

Later this week, I wish to see him in a good mental state, like the days we were sharing a bedroom as kids.

We speak episodically or based on calendar rituals. Birthdays. Easter. Christmas. New Year.

It's getting better.

I love my brother, but he scares me. He speaks more about death than the joy of life. I worry he'll commit suicide.

Dad tried twice. That I know of. Acknowledging two was enough for me.

I remember vividly his scratched, blue-red-purple throat. It's very hard to hide a bruised neck.

The first time around, he chickened out. Maybe he realised the gift of life. Whatever it was, it was a bad show.

The second time around, it was me who cut the rope.

Talking of madness, nothing can beat the day my dad fired his gun inside the kitchen at 6:00 a.m. Only Mum was with him in the room. We, my siblings and I, were still in bed sleeping. Waking up to the noise and smell of gunpowder is awful. Inhuman.

My heart was racing madly. My head couldn't comprehend.
I still don't understand.

Was it a distress call? A botched suicide attempt? Was he
aiming at Mum? Did Mum save his life?

Or was it the other way around? Did he save her? Did Mum
try to commit suicide?

This thought doesn't sit well with me.

How can a mother of four want to kill herself?

Despair, maybe?

Burnout?

Poor life choices?

Forced marriage?

Enough black eyes?

Maybe she couldn't run away.

Maybe she didn't know she was allowed to run away.

To breathe.

To reassess.

To make new choices.

It was her right.

Sadly, no one told her.

Another generation. Another education.

Ostend wasn't far.

Even for an hour or two.

She tried once to escape her mundane life.

She slammed the house front door with great brutality, only to be back soon later.

She simply walked around the block.

There was nowhere to go.

She was an orphan at sixteen.

A life weight she doesn't want to let go of.

An endless parody highlighted in all her adult conversations.

Being an orphan is painful, but rejection is worse.

She was emancipated after her mum's passing.

No one wanted her.

She was ousted. Kicked out. Alone.

With an anger to prove her worth, she raised her family based on appearance.

We are the projection of her ideals.

A nightmare behind closed doors.

A place where authenticity isn't welcome.

A fake living standard where displays of love and affection weren't priorities.

She survived her loss through a mad dream.

Filled with verbal and physical violence.

As a kid, I dreamt of running away day and night.

Now, I am her runaway boy—a runaway man.

The edge of my mental cliff compels me to run away.

My back cold against the metal bench, I sit with my millions of questions that no one—including myself—can answer.

Coming back to Belgium is a painful pilgrimage. An agony. A sweet and sour delicatessen.

Ostend is the sweet part of the dish.

The man who triggered my mental interlude has disappeared into the crowd. He is nowhere to be seen. I'd had enough of him anyway. I needed joy and happiness.

My footsteps took me to a tiny art supply shop that smelled of linseed oil, turpentine and acrylic paints. I felt instantly connected to my wife and daughter.

Both were born with a paintbrush and a ceramic knife in their hands. Painting, sculpture, illustration, literature and music are the core languages of our household—and gaming, for my son. These magical languages are the gateway to our individual and collective sanities.

I bought a postcard I didn't need. A photo of the beach with storm clouds above it. It felt honest. It felt raw. It felt like me.

Back in the flat, I wrote on the back:

> *Greg,*
>
> *I saw you today.*
>
> *Except it wasn't you.*
>
> *Wish it had been.*
>
> *In my vision, your lungs were filled with joy.*
>
> *Your eyes were full of light.*
>
> *Love,*
>
> *Your brother.*
>
> *Maxsense.*

I didn't post it. I had no postal stamps to lick.

I placed it in my suitcase, where all the things that make no sense seem to end up.

That night, my dreams brought me to the church.

The same stillness greeted me. A soft rustle of coats and low voices. A few candles flickering near the mosaic. I didn't say a word or a prayer. Just lit a flame and stood there breathing calmly.

Greg was there too. Laughing at me for going soft in a church. He stood behind me, hands jammed in his pockets, and said,

"Are you free? Are you happy now?"

The candles answered on my behalf through the grace of their sensual dancing and the heart-warming murmur of their silent talking.

Seeing that I didn't want to dance with him, Greg left.

There is no happiness in trauma. Only rare bursts of enlightenment.

Fronting Mary, I confessed quietly that it's hard to be me.

I don't know why, I added, my reactive behaviour can be labelled as one-third defensive, one-third exposed, one-sixth romantic and one-sixth melancholic.

Chapter 4

Candles and Currency

In front of the statue of Mary, there's a black minimalist candle rack that looks like something out of a funeral catalogue. A small steel box with a slot accepting donations is attached to it. A faded sticker inviting holy consumption reads: €2 and €5.

Two euros is for the regular-sized candle, and five euros is for the big one. The cost of inflation is included. Whatever—if size matters in the miracle world, that's the going rate for a flicker of hope.

It's not official, of course. There's no priest standing by watching you empty your purse or pockets. Whatever you do, always remember that cash is king for Mary.

People treat the candle distributor like a sacred vending

machine. Insert coin. Select miracle. Terms and conditions apply.

One bloke, maybe sixty, fumbled through his pockets for ages before dropping in a button. A button. Then he lit the candle and stood there like he'd paid full price. I didn't know if I admired him or felt sorry for him. Mary didn't seem to mind.

A lady came in with a purse full of coins and lit five candles in a row. She lit one for her son, one for her marriage, one for her dog, and two for "just in case." She looked exhausted— like life had worn through her edges.

Then came a student who clearly hadn't read the sign. He stood in front of the machine, sighed, and tapped his phone against the donation slot. Nothing happened. He shrugged and lit a candle anyway. Faith, it seems, is contactless now.

The whole ritual fascinated me. The exchange. The idea that somewhere, someone decided €2 was the price of divine attention. As if heaven accepted small change and receipts.

I imagined Mary keeping a ledger and heading the holy promotions department.

"Today's deal: three prayers for healing, two for love, one for revenge, and only €19.99. No more to pay. Just walk away."

And yet, there was something deeply human about it. Even the absurdity held weight. People gave what they could. Not just money—time, silence, hope. It wasn't about the coins or the notes. It was about the pause. That moment where someone said, I'm not in control, and I still believe.

Well, almost believe.

I watched a man light a candle and then immediately blow it out, whispering, "Nah, stupid." He walked off before the smoke cleared.

What was he thinking? There's nothing to lose, but plenty to gain.

Then there was the tourist who lit a candle and took a selfie with it, adding a filter that made her face glow like a saint. She smiled at the statue, thanked it in English, and left behind a postcard that said: "Sending prayers from Belgium!"

I sat behind them all, keyboarding on my phone, feeling like I was eavesdropping on souls.

And Mary stood there, as always—unmoved but not uncaring. Her face was unreadable. She might've been weeping. Or smiling. Or both.

When I finally got up to leave, I dropped two euros in the box, lit a candle, and didn't ask for anything. Just stood there with my hands in my coat pockets, thinking about buttons and phone taps and that woman who lit candles "just in case."

That felt good—and cheap—considering the entertainment.

Midway through the nave, I traced my steps back, dropped another four euros in the miracle slot, and lit one candle for my parents and siblings and another for my wife and children.

"Many blessings" were my words.

Chapter 5

My Hoodie Is Gone

It was another type of those machines that eats coins and memories.

I stood at the laundrette on Van Iseghemlaan, half-asleep and holding a plastic tub of clothes like it contained secrets. The machines were humming their usual sad little rotary tune. I was the only one there apart from a man reading the sports pages, muttering in Flemish, and drinking a Jupiler. A man's beer, as stated in their early days marketing campaign.

I loaded my things: two shirts, socks, jeans, the royal blue hoodie I always packed even when I promised myself I wouldn't.

The machine whirred to life.

I walked to the bakery next door for a coffee and came back

twenty minutes later.

The washer was open—a few things were gone.

Not the whole load—just a few items: one T-shirt, some socks, and the hoodie.

I frantically checked the machine. Checked the other machines. Checked the dryer. Checked the floor. Nothing.

Someone had opened the washer while I was gone and taken what they liked.

I let out a string of profanities. It was more than a string.

The man with the newspaper shrugged.

"It happens sometimes," he said.

I thanked him for the insight and kept my mouth shut about his inaction. He could have done something. Or maybe not. I shouldn't speculate on his performance. Could I have done something better? Only God knows.

I stood there longer than I should've. Just staring into the half-empty drum.

And that's when it hit me.

My hoodie was gone. For good.

No ceremony. No goodbye. No folded farewell. Just—taken.

I sat down on the plastic chair next to the window. Didn't cry. Didn't curse anyone. Simply clenched my teeth unconsciously before I felt the ache crawl up my arms and settle somewhere behind my ribs.

I felt stabbed. Used. And abused.

It wasn't just about the hoodie.

It was about all the things I'd lost quietly. All the parts of me that had been peeled off slowly over the years—relationships, cities, pieces of self-trust—and how I never really gave myself permission to grieve them.

That soft cotton hoodie—a cosy emotional sleeping bag, friction wear marks around the cuffs, hood drawstring missing. Smelled of travels, airport floors, connection anxiety, and whatever detergent we used at home.

That hoodie saw me through more than most people did.

It experienced my endless 18-month work cycles, my yearly trip to Belgium.

It knew the weight of nights I didn't want to wake up from. It had absorbed tears I didn't admit to. It had sat with me on fire escapes, in airport lounges, on therapists' couches, in hospital waiting rooms, on floors I didn't plan to sleep on.

It lit candles with me in Ostend, Banneux, Tancrémont, and other parts of the world.

It was a bloody holy hoodie, I know. But grief doesn't always cling to what makes sense.

I just kept moving forward. Drying, folding, packing.

That afternoon, I walked aimlessly through town, half-watching tourists take selfies with Belgian waffles. I ended up on the beach, sitting in the wind with a coffee that tasted like a jar of festering irritation.

I imagined the hoodie out in the world—maybe on someone who needed it more. Maybe draped across a chair in a café. Maybe dumped in a bin, forgotten like an old receipt.

I whispered goodbye anyway.

That evening, I purchased a candle at the supermarket.

I lit it. Not for the hoodie but for what it held. My runaway episodes.

The version of me that wore it—afraid, cracked open, surviving on hope, lukewarm emotions, hot chips, frikandel, andalouse sauce, and Lindemans Kriek.

I let that version go with the flame.

And for the first time in years, I didn't wrap myself in something familiar.

Novelty is hard to embrace.

Chapter 6

The First Whisper

I didn't hear it at first. Not clearly.

It was just a flicker, like the tail end of someone else's sentence drifting across the pews. I looked around. No one near me. The only other person in the church was an old man in a beige overcoat, mumbling into his scarf as he lit a candle and shuffled away.

Then it came again. A whisper, soft but sharp, like someone telling a secret they weren't supposed to say out loud.

"You've been watching too long. Say something."

I froze. Not out of fear. More... embarrassment? Like when you realise someone's been reading over your shoulder. Except I was the only one there.

I looked at the statue of Mary. She didn't move, obviously. Her mosaic face glowed gently in the mid-afternoon light, lips tilted somewhere between mercy and boredom.

"Right," I muttered, rubbing my temples. "Lack of caffeine. Or sleep. Or both."

I stood up to leave and heard it again.

"Chicken."

It wasn't cruel. If anything, it was... cheeky. Like a younger sibling daring you to jump off the swing.

"Excuse me?" I whispered, suddenly aware I was speaking to empty space. "If that was divine communication, you might want to workshop the tone."

No reply.

I walked outside, stared up at the spires, and wondered if pigeons ever felt chosen.

But something itched. Not in my body—in the air. Like when you're about to be rained on, but the clouds haven't made up their minds yet.

The next day, I went back. Lit a candle—just one—and sat in the same chair as before: the second one from the right in the front row. No whisper. No voice. Just me.

I played another levitation game with the statue of Saint Thérèse of Lisieux. Our eyes locked with softness. An imaginative smile carved her womanly lips. The blue and red lights of the stained-glass windows made her float for a fraction of a second.

When my mind acknowledged what had just happened, my hara energy traversed my body at the speed of light and delivered a loud—orgasmic-like—spasm.

I checked around to see if anyone had seen me. I was alone in the church, but I had the strange feeling someone was watching me now—not judging, just... waiting.

As I left, I passed the black steel candle stand and heard it again. Not with my ears exactly—in my chest. Deep in the middle.

"Took you long enough."

I didn't look back. I just smiled, like someone who's just been handed a map for a place that doesn't exist yet.

And for the first time since I started sitting in that church, I wasn't just observing anymore. I was... involved.

TWO EURO CANDLES

Chapter 7

A Life Filled With Lies

His face is familiar. I see him once a year. He is part of Ostend's living landscape. He's the lead singer of a Bob Marley tribute band—and now, he's also the cleaner of the venue that once let him chase smoke, skin, and sound late into the night. Only the smell of old beer, cold cigarettes, urine, and vomit welcomes his day.

Today, I caught him crying like a child while rearranging the tables and chairs on the terrace outside the venue. It was more than a big cry. It was the end of the world—the end of his world.

I approached him, checking on his welfare and offering reassurance.

His mama had died a couple of days ago in his faraway land

called Jamaica. He had no money to make the trip back to Kingston. She'd had a heart attack. In a few seconds, I knew his life, his sorrows, and his despair.

His posture wasn't that of a lead singer swaggering in front of women at night—it was the posture of a broken boy, lost in a cold seaside town far away from the land of Exodus. His world-touring dream had made him a broke man.

"I haven't got money. Just five euros in my pocket!" he repeated.

Reality had caught up with him. The Rasta lifestyle wasn't sweet anymore.

I told him that five euros is all it takes to celebrate his mum's life. I invited him to visit Mary at the church and to purchase a candle, some time alone, and silence.

I don't know if he listened, acted, or committed to my words. That was the only thing I could offer—with my limited skills and resources. But all day, my thoughts were with him, and at night I typed a journal entry for him and his mother. Both deserved some cinematic choreography. Some distorted truths.

> *Rain lashed down on the slate roof as he stepped inside, the cold stone beneath his feet sending a jolt through his soles. He exhaled long and low—the breath of a man carrying too many years and too little clarity. The wooden door closed behind him with a soft but deliberate thud, muffling the thunder and shutting out the grey skies of Ostend.*

He paused just inside, letting the scent of the place wrap around him. Wax and old stone. The ghost of incense still lingering in the rafters. A smell that belonged nowhere near a man like him—but today, somehow, it called him.

He stood over six feet tall, though the slump in his shoulders made him seem smaller. His dreadlocks fell in thick ropes to the middle of his back, rain-speckled and still dripping. He wore an old army-green jacket over a knitted jumper in bold Rasta colours—red, gold, green—the threads thinning near the cuffs. His jeans sagged, heavy with water, and his shoes squeaked against the polished floor. He looked like a ghost of himself. Not the stage lion, not the voice of thunder, not the man who made women laugh and sway. Just a man now. Just a son.

He shuffled forward slowly, hands buried in the pockets of his jacket. One clutched a guitar pick, the other a crumpled five-euro note, now dry but limp from being folded and unfolded too many times. He glanced around the nave without moving his head too much, hoping no one recognised him. No one did. His night fans were still asleep at this time of day. Only a few scattered tourists, heads bowed or eyes closed. The stained-glass windows cast polychromatic light through the rain, painting the stone columns with watery patterns of ruby, emerald, and sapphire.

As he turned into the left aisle, he saw her—Mary.

She was pale in the mosaic, glowing like moonlight in a field of frost. Her arms stretched wide—not demanding, not beckoning— just open. There was something in her stillness that made his ribs ache.

In front of her, the black steel candle stand looked like a lightweight edifice. A few small flames flickered—each one a story, a sorrow, a plea. He hesitated. He looked at Mary again and took another step forward.

His hand reached slowly into his pocket. Not the side with the pick. The other one. He pulled out the five-euro note and stared at it for a second, thumb brushing its ridged edge. Five euros. A tiny meal. A tram ticket. Two beers during happy hour. A third of a night and a shower in a youth hostel. Or—one candle.

He chose the candle.

He slid the note into the slot. It rang silent in the steel box. Then he picked the largest candle he could find—thick and tall, like it should last longer than all the others. Using the flame of another candle, it took him no time to light. The flame burned—steady, silent, pure.

He bent his head forward and whispered something—not to Mary exactly. To his mother.

He felt ashamed to be in this strange, wet place, singing Bob Marley tributes to crowds who didn't even know his name. He felt regret that he hadn't even been able to afford the flight home. While biting his fingernails, he realised that she had been the only steady voice in the background of his chaos. And now, she was gone.

He closed his eyes.

"Mama," he whispered. "Dis one for you."

He pulled a crumpled slip of paper from his back pocket. It was damp, the ink smudged, but the words were still legible. A song. His song. All inspired by Bob Marley's words, lyrics, and colourful aura. He'd probably written it the night she died—locked in the shared bathroom of a hostel, crying into his knees while the world outside cheered another chorus of Redemption Song. This one wasn't for the crowd.

One Life (Mama's Song)

One life, mama, you gave me one life

Fed me truth through struggle and strife

You were the calm in the lion's roar

Now your voice doesn't sing no more

One love, you said it with your eyes

Held me close when I told too many lies

And now the wind carries your name

But the house doesn't feel the same

So I light dis flame for the tears you cried

For the prayers you prayed, and the nights you tried

I light dis flame for the road I roam

'Cause every road still lead me home

One life, mama, you gave me light

Through the Babylon dark and the preacher's fight

And though your body sleep back in the land

Your song still holds me hand

His voice cracked when he read the last line. Not like on stage. Not show business-like. Just cracked. Raw. Like an open wound.

He sat down in the pew before Mary, paper in hand, head bowed low. No swagger. Just sweat and grief and the scent of rain and old churches around him. He didn't cross himself. But he held the candle in his eyes like it was burning for real.

Outside, the storm had begun to ease. The patter of rain softened. Light broke briefly through the grey, and the glass above Mary's head blazed gold for one fleeting second.

He felt it on his face and closed his eyes again.

Then, gently, he stood.

He looked once more at Mary—not in search of answers, but for something quieter. A nod of thanks. Or understanding.

As soon as I finished my journal entry, my thoughts drifted. I began to wonder what kind of emotions or reactions I'll have the day my parents pass away. Writing those lines made me realise that I, too, am living in exile—and perhaps, just perhaps, I won't even have the money for a plane ticket. Could closure be achieved through a candle or two?

But closure won't come unless I know my parents intimately.

I know their reactive behaviours, their facades, the way they rewrite their life story as they breathe, the countless lies, the subjects they avoid, the superficial masks, their individual and shared control patterns, and all the tools they use to disguise and camouflage their feelings and emotional burdens.

Wouldn't it be something to hear them speak about their pain and trauma in their own words?

To see their faces as they attempt honesty.

To acknowledge their mess and misery—not with judgement, but as part of their human truth.

My quest for authenticity has often made me feel like a failure on legs. It's cost me everything. I've self-sabotaged. But I hold no shame. I've learnt how to bounce back. It's painful, dramatic, expensive on all levels—but necessary.

I'd be curious to know how my mum felt when she stood as a human shield between her raging husband and me.

Even more so, I'd like to understand what thoughts led a father to press a 9 mm loaded gun to his son's head—or to strangle his daughter over a petty act of teenage disobedience.

As children of the war—born in 1940 and 1944—what did they experience as kids? As teenagers?

What truly made my father run away from home and join the military police at sixteen?

I don't want psychological theories.

I'm not seeking therapy.

I want their voices—the ones from deep inside.

The voices they've silenced to keep up appearances.

That silent behaviour that breeds division, tension, and isolation.

It won't happen. I know that. And it hurts.

But the question lingers.

Who are they, really?

And by extension—who am I?

How many lies have I told just to survive? Just to become invisible?

How many lies have I spun over the years to embellish my story, conceal truths, or build and protect the persona I call me?

Emotional survival often begins with a lie. But did it have to?

How many relationships have I lost because of my emotional dishonesty?

How many of those lies still live inside me—truths I'll never be able to voice or purge? Not because I'm unwilling, but because they're buried too deep to reach.

TWO EURO CANDLES

Chapter 8

Is That You, Little Flower?

"Saint Thérèse of Lisieux," the whisper said, as if it was obvious.

Then added, almost smugly: "But you can call me Thérèse. No need for the halos."

I blinked. Literally blinked. Like someone had just thrown glitter in my face.

"You what?"

"Saint. Thérèse. Of Lisieux." She spoke slowly, as if I were thick. "You know—the one with the roses, the convent, the tuberculosis. Bit of a hit of Normandy. Your levitation pleasure."

I sat back in the chair, heart ticking faster.

Of all the holy figures I could've hallucinated, I got the patron saint of floral metaphors and dying young?

"Why me?" I asked aloud.

Silence.

Then: "Because you're paying attention. Sort of."

There was a pause. I waited. She waited. We waited.

"Am I losing it?" I muttered.

"You'd be surprised how often people ask that right before something wonderful happens."

Her voice wasn't booming. No thunder. No echoes. Just a soft, familiar cadence that sat in the back of your mind like a song lyric you didn't know you knew. It was warm. Slightly amused. Definitely female. Somewhere between your favourite teacher and someone who could convincingly steal a library book and get away with it.

"So. Let me guess," she said. "You've been watching people light candles, scribbling in that electronic pocket notebook of yours, pretending you're not waiting for something."

I glanced down at my notes. They suddenly felt flimsy.

"You're not wrong," I admitted. "But I didn't expect—this."

"No one does. That's sort of the point."

I looked around. A few tourists shuffled in, blinking at the stained glass, mumbling about how 'Instagram didn't do it justice'. I lowered my head and whispered, "This is either divine contact or a psychotic break."

"Let's say it's both," Thérèse replied brightly. "Life's more interesting that way."

She was nothing like the statues or prayer cards. No syrupy solemnity. No gold-embossed suffering. Just quick wit and something else under it—something old and wise and wildly playful, like my levitation game.

"Shouldn't you be... solemn?" I asked.

"Oh, absolutely not," she said. "God has plenty of serious types. I got this gig because I made Him laugh."

I couldn't help it. I laughed too. Out loud. A good deep honest laugh with silly tears joining the party.

A woman two rows behind looked at me like I'd just farted during Mass. My foreigner behaviour didn't impress her.

"Look," Thérèse continued, "you've come here every day, watching people beg for impossible things. And you think they're somehow all cracked in the head. But the thing is, you're here too. And whether you admit it or not, you want something."

I swallowed. "Yeah. Well. Don't we all?"

"Exactly." Her voice softened. "Now let's find out what your something is."

The candles flickered. The sun's reflection hit the mosaic

just right. For a moment, it looked like Mary winked.

Chapter 9

Cheese Sandwiches And The Universe

It was never meant to mean anything.

Just a cheese sandwich.

I'd wandered into the bakery on a cold afternoon after walking too long in shoes that weren't made for real distance—the kind of tired that starts in your ankles and ends in your soul. I'd passed three cafés that looked too full, two that looked too empty, and finally ducked into a place that smelled like warm butter and something quietly holy.

There was a queue. Locals, mostly. No menus on the walls. Just a glass case filled with dough and promise.

When it was my turn, I panicked.

I asked—in a bad French-English blend—what was simple.

The woman behind the counter smiled, soft as cotton. She didn't speak much English, but she said, "Fromage. Pain. Warm?"

"Yes," I said. "Oui, merci."

She nodded and turned. I watched her assemble it like she was building a memory. Slow. Generous. A little too much cheese. Just right.

She wrapped it in paper like she was tucking a newborn into bed.

When she handed it over, she said something I didn't catch. But her tone—it felt like care. Like she didn't just want me to eat. She wanted me to be nourished.

I took the sandwich to the park near the Leopold Hotel. Found a bench that didn't have seagull droppings on it. Unwrapped it carefully, like I was opening something sacred.

First bite: creamy, bitey walnut cheese and fresh, crusty bread that pulled my gustatory system to heaven. I closed my eyes.

It hit me. The strangest, deepest wave of... something. Gratitude? Abundance?

It felt like a late-night meal prepared by my newlywed wife years ago. I could taste the care and love—something I'd become accustomed to over the years, but that was still served, meal after meal, whatever the day of the week. I felt instantly blessed and privileged by the small things in life that make our existence a joyful experience.

The sandwich was gone in five minutes.

But the emotional savour it left behind—stayed.

I went back the next day to thank the woman.

The sandwich lady wasn't there.

Someone else behind the counter. Same bread, different hands.

That's how it works, I think.

Miracles don't always hang around.

Sometimes they show up in a strange form, do what they need to do, and disappear before you get a chance to say thank you.

TWO EURO CANDLES

Chapter 10

I'm Not Religious

"Thérèse, I'm not religious," I told her.

"You say that like it's meant to impress me."

Thérèse's voice came with a smile I could feel. Not smug, just knowing. Like someone who's heard every excuse in the book and still has time for tea.

"I was forced into it," I admitted. "No practising generational Catholic. Weird heritage. We celebrated Christmas for the presents and Easter for the chocolate eggs. I was dipped into the holy water at birth—sorry, you call it christening—like all the previous non-believing generations before me. My siblings and I were forced into two rounds of communion to keep up with the Joneses. This Catholic episode cost me a slap in the face by the local priest for ringing the holy bells too long for his liking. How can I believe in God after that?"

"Mmm," she hummed.

"My mischief was often blessed with a bucket of guilt and sentences straight out of an exorcism book when my mother's patience ran dry. I was acknowledged as the devil's child or a bastard before a wooden spoon broke on my back or skull."

"A classic vintage. Not really funny, but still funny in many ways."

I leaned back in the pew, arms folded. "I never prayed when I was young. I was too busy worrying about my safety, or keeping an eye on the household madness. Even if I had prayed, there wasn't any guarantee it would've worked."

"Depends what you mean by 'worked'."

"I mean... He never showed up. Not for me. Not when I needed it. Not when hands became fists and words became insults."

Thérèse didn't flinch. Didn't defend God. Didn't justify the silence. Just let me sit with the words.

"I get it," she said eventually. "You think if God really cared, He wouldn't have let you grow up with all that ache."

I nodded.

"Well, spoiler alert: He did care. He just didn't think your life should be a curated Instagram feed."

I barked out a laugh. "That's the best divine apology I've ever heard."

She chuckled too. "Who said it was an apology?"

"My life wasn't a divine experience—more a rollercoaster from hell," I said resentfully.

I sat with that. Let it sting a bit. Let it settle.

But my raw emotional impulses couldn't cope with just being an observer. I needed to join the dance floor of my life's misery, so I added, "I still don't buy the whole system. Prayer lines, saints, blessings—it all feels like slot machines and sweet talk."

Thérèse's voice lowered, more serious now. "That's fine. Don't buy the system. Just look at the people. Look at them come in here with their doubt and damage, and still... ask."

"I looked. I've been looking. I've begged all my life to experience some form of normality—not the extremes of life," I whispered.

"Do you know what I see?" Thérèse asked. "Someone who's been disappointed by life, maybe by God—but still came back to say hello."

I didn't reply. My throat had that tight feeling you get before a tear decides if it's showing up or not.

"I never asked you to believe everything," she added. "Just be honest about what you do."

I looked up at the mosaic of Mary. She seemed softer today. Or maybe I was just seeing her properly for the first time.

I whispered, "I'm here, aren't I?"

"That's faith, darling," Thérèse said. "You're already in it."

Chapter 11

A Seagull

I didn't notice it at first.

Just a white smudge on the balcony rail. Could've been a shadow, could've been the wind playing tricks. But then it moved. Looked straight at me. Blinked—twice. Settled in.

A seagull.

Not remarkable. Not majestic. Just an overweight seagull.

I waved my hand. It didn't budge.

I tapped the glass. Nothing.

"Shoo," I said aloud, more from habit than expectation. It tilted its head as if I'd just said something offensive in a language it didn't respect.

That was Day One.

By Day Three, it was still there.

Same spot on the railing. Rain or no rain. In the morning, when I made tea. In the evening, when I stared out at the street trying to remember why I came to Ostend in the first place.

I googled "how to get rid of seagulls." The answers ranged from "tinfoil" to "fake owls" to "spiritual surrender."

I had none of those. So I tried bread.

It didn't take the bait.

Just blinked again. Twice. Then fluttered and fluffed its feathers like someone settling in for a long appointment.

Eventually, I gave up. Started greeting it in the morning.

"Morning, mate."

Sometimes it squawked. Sometimes not.

I started talking to it. Small things. Stupid things—Like I did with my late dog—Buddy.

Told it I once wanted to be a pastry chef but failed to overcome my father's objections. Told it about a girl who kicked the door of my white Ford Fiesta. Told it about the job I left without warning after the company induction tour was over. Told it I became an architect to prove to my father that I wasn't an idiot. Told it about a novel I wrote that gave me grief after reading an article about it in a national newspaper.

The seagull never interrupted.

Just listened, in that infuriating way seagulls do—like they're barely tolerating your presence but willing to humour you.

On Day Five, it was raining sideways. I expected it to be gone.

But there it was, soaked and defiant.

That did something to me.

I sat at the tiny dining table in the Airbnb and cried. Nothing cinematic. Just a slow, wet unravel that started in the throat and ended somewhere in the centre of my chest.

When I looked up, the seagull was still watching.

"Don't judge me," I muttered.

It blinked again.

I could've sworn it nodded.

Later that week, it left. Just… wasn't there anymore. No fanfare. No trace. Just an empty railing and the faint disappointment of being abandoned by someone you never admitted you liked.

But here's the thing—since it left, I've kept talking.

To no one. To the universe.

Turns out, I needed a listener more than a solution.

Chapter 12

Be Specific

He came in wearing a tracksuit that had seen better decades, hair slicked back with something halfway between gel and desperation. Late fifties, maybe early sixties. The type of bloke who's probably told the same pub joke for thirty years and still laughs first.

He walked up to the candle stand like it was a pokies machine. Dug around in his pocket, pulled out a gold coin with a little ceremony, and dropped it into the slot.

Then, very seriously, very softly, he said: "Mary, I'm done with the gambling. I need a dog. A loyal one. Not too yappy. Amen."

I blinked. Did I hear that right?

Thérèse let out a delighted little gasp in my mind. "Finally!

A specific request."

He lit the candle. Stepped back. Nodded like a poker hand had been made. Then walked straight out. No hesitation. No lingering. Just business done.

"Did he just ask Mary for a dog to help him quit gambling?" I muttered.

"Oh, absolutely," said Thérèse. "And I admire the clarity. Faith with a touch of consumer confidence."

The next day, he was back. This time with a Jack Russell on a lead. It trotted beside him like it had belonged to him in a previous life.

"Voilà," he said to no one in particular. "She came to me outside—at the wharf. No collar. Just jumped at me. I wrapped her in my jacket."

He lit another candle, tossed in a coin, and whispered, "Finder keeper. If that's alright with Mary."

I stared. The dog barked once, then sat. Like it was joining in.

"Maybe it's just coincidence," I said, half to Thérèse, half to myself.

"Sure," she replied. "And maybe Noah's Ark is berthed in town for the weekend."

He stood there patting the dog, eyes damp but proud. I swear the candle burned just a little brighter next to him.

It wasn't a big thing. Not a healing. Not a lightning bolt. Just a bloke, a promise, and a small dog with one ear that didn't sit right.

Still, something in me shifted. Not because the miracle had "worked", but because he believed it had. Because belief—even ridiculous belief—changes how people walk.

And honestly—if a miracle comes with a wagging tail and a few less playing card shuffles and lottery tickets, who am I to argue?

My mind spun like a washing machine drum.

If miracles are rewarded based on their specificities—could someone put a label on the candle holder, stating in big capital letters: BE SPECIFIC?

Through my personal journey, I've learned to manifest, to desire, and to embody a wanted reality before it becomes my new reality.

After checking in with Thérèse—not to levitate her, but to get feedback on my insight—I grabbed my phone and wrote:

> *Thérèse won't speak in today's self-help or manifestation language, but her "Little Way" actually aligns deeply with the idea of embodying one's deepest desires—not through ambition or grand plans, but through simple, persistent love and trust.*
>
> *She believed our desires, especially the pure and holy ones, are planted in us by God.*

I could hear her saying—"God would not inspire us with desires which cannot be realised."

I acknowledged the power contained in her words. I kept still for a while, reflecting on my manifestation and the life I design.

My fingers couldn't stay still and added:

> *If you have a deep longing within you—especially one rooted in love, service, or creativity—then you can trust that it's not only valid, but meant to become real in some way.*
>
> *Having gained some understanding of her way of living through her letters, Thérèse "visualised" her dreams not with vision boards or affirmations, but through prayer, surrender, and childlike confidence in God's love. She imagined herself doing great things for God, and even when she couldn't physically achieve them, she trusted that her desire itself was meaningful and fruitful.*

As I was ready to leave, Thérèse whispered:

"If your dream is born from love, embody it with your whole heart—even in the smallest acts—and trust that it is already real in God's eyes."

I smiled. I glowed.

My favourite sentence has always been—I put my heart in my doing.

Out of the church, I looked around to see the dog God brought in. I couldn't believe it—it was a perfect replica of

Buddy, my late Jack Russell.

I missed my dog.

I missed our stupid conversations and his bad juvenile behaviour.

TWO EURO CANDLES

Chapter 13

Riesling

It happened in a small bar tucked down a side street behind the casino.

Not the sort of place you plan to find—just the kind of door you try when you've had enough of the North Sea winds chiselling your face with their arctic cold, or when you don't feel like sitting in your own silence anymore.

The bar was half-lit, all wood and whispers, the kind of joint where the chairs don't match and the wine list is two reds and a white scribbled on a chalkboard. I ordered something I could pronounce—a Campari orange—and made my way to a corner table with a wobble in the leg and the cloud of someone else's cigarette in the air.

That's when she arrived, aiming for the same table.

Mid-sixties. Hair like the inside of a seashell. Long coat that looked like it had stories sewn into the seams. She saw me, froze for half a second, and then something cracked across her face—joy, disbelief, grief? I still can't say.

"Lionel?" she asked.

I opened my mouth to correct her, but she was already moving—arms out, trembling smile, tears in her eyes.

Before I could stop her, she wrapped me in a hug that didn't feel like a mistake.

I stood there, arms stiff, until instinct kicked in and I hugged her back.

She pulled away, hands on my shoulders, studying my face like a map she hadn't seen since the war.

"My God," she whispered. "You came back."

I didn't know what to say.

So I didn't.

She sat. I sat. Two chipped glasses of Riesling appeared. The bartender nodded in silence. I returned the nod, quietly acknowledging that my Campari orange would be a miss.

She talked.

Not to me exactly—but to the memory I now resembled. Just as I did with my brother a few days ago. She told me about the street she used to live on. The cat that died last winter. The cousin who never apologised. The man she once loved who disappeared into himself after their daughter died.

And I listened.

I nodded in approval.

Because something about her sadness and authenticity felt familiar. Like we'd both been carrying it in different colours.

At some point, I said, "I'm not Lionel."

She smiled—gentle, knowing.

"I know."

I blinked. "Why did you hug me?"

"Because I needed to," she said. "And you didn't stop me."

We sat in silence after that. Just sipped. Just breathed. Just existed.

The wine was ordinary. The glass chipped.

But it tasted like something kind.

A gentle life-sweetener. A reminder of God's abundance.

When she left, she kissed me on the forehead. No performance. No confusion.

"Thank you," she said.

"For what?"

"For not breaking the moment."

That night, back at the flat, I stood in front of the mirror and tried to imagine being Lionel. Who he was. What he did. Why he left. Did he leave?

Then I looked closer—and saw myself differently.

Not as a mistake.

But as someone who, just for one night, stepped into the space love had left behind, I sat on the bed and asked myself a touchy question: "Where love used to live?"

Louis, Franco, and Bruna came to mind.

Three life angels. Three life mentors.

All three led me to discover and experience, in different ways, the value of life—and my own value. I was barely sixteen years old at the time.

They were ordinary people doing ordinary things—but when they took me under their wings, I flew. I flew high. I flew to the point of no return. I became a man. Young, but a man.

It was more that a rite of passage.

I felt love—the unconditional paternal and maternal kind.

The one that costs nothing to give or receive.

Under Louis' wing, I learned the woodworking craft—the traditional way. All by hand. No power tools. Blisters, sweat, and sharp chisels. From design to installation. A harsh world of crafted precision, yielding endless satisfaction upon completion.

Bruna and Franco—unrelated, yet united by a shared passion for Italian culture and life.

Under their wings, I learned the refined skills of a five-star hotel barman.

Refinement at its best.

Dressed in a million-dollar uniform, I grew into presence, humility, and courtesy.

I took pride in being part of a frivolous world of wealth and perfection.

All three lived ordinary lives with ordinary problems—yet they still took the time to invite me to find myself.

The conversations were unlike anything I'd experienced at home.

I was valued. And I valued them.

We complemented each other like a match made in heaven.

Bruna couldn't help but guide my love life and introduce me to the power of self-healing.

Business and entrepreneurship were Louis' forte.

Franco, a true Italian stallion, lectured me on sex education—in his imaginative Aldo Maccione way. His mantra was simple: "Never in the bedroom."

Tonight, it's bittersweet.

Louis and Franco are in heaven, and Bruna has dementia.

Their skills, intellect, mannerisms, and humour live on in me.

This is where love is.

True love that makes my eyes red and pearly.

Under their wings, I was blessed. Privileged. Conscientious.

Today, I remain blessed, privileged, and conscientious.

Chapter 14

Thérèse Likes Jokes

"I thought saints were meant to be solemn," I said, knowing well that I repeated myself.

"You thought wrong," Thérèse replied—and I swear I could hear her grinning.

We'd fallen into the habit of chatting. Not every day, and not always in full sentences. Sometimes she'd drop in like a breeze, just a word or two. Other days, I'd sit in silence, unsure if I was praying or just having a slow conversation with someone who happened to be dead.

But today, she was in a playful mood.

"Do you know," she said, "I once snuck honey into the convent kitchen to sweeten the lentils. The others thought it was divine intervention. I let them."

"You were a saint and a prankster?"

"I was fourteen in a room full of nuns with no sugar. What did you expect?"

She told me stories. Real ones. Like how she once fell asleep mid-prayer and drooled on her breviary. Or how she hated loud chewing during silence, and once faked a coughing fit to drown it out.

"And you were canonised?"

"Holiness isn't about being humourless. It's about being real. God made laughter, too. Don't pretend it's not holy."

I didn't know whether to laugh or light a candle in her honour.

I laughed.

Outside, a dog barked. Inside, someone knocked over a candle and nearly set their scarf on fire. Nobody screamed. A woman simply stamped it out with the calm of someone who's raised four sons, survived three divorces and breast cancer.

Thérèse giggled. "See? Saints in the making."

I leaned back in the chair. The church was quieter than usual. Still, somehow, it felt full in my head.

I looked at the statue of Mary and asked, "Do you think she ever laughed?"

"She laughs constantly," said Thérèse. "Usually at the same

things you do."

The idea of Mary chuckling at humans lighting candles like they're lodging customer complaints made me smile. Maybe that was the whole point—taking the sacred less seriously without making it less sacred.

I didn't know if that would work, but it felt like a beautiful philosophy.

"Can I ask you something?" I said.

"Always."

"Why me?"

She paused. The longest pause she'd ever given.

"Because you needed to be reminded that joy is a kind of faith. And because I like the way your mind bends when you're not trying to impress anyone, or to fit in, disappear, or run away."

I didn't know what to say to that. So I said nothing. Just sat there, in the glow of candles, the weight of silence, and the strange comfort of being slightly cracked open.

Before I left, I lit a candle. Not for anyone. Not for anything.

Just because it felt good. Joyful even.

Outside, I couldn't stop thinking about taking the sacred less seriously without making it less sacred.

I couldn't help myself—my phone keyboard was ready to

record my oncoming thoughts.

Control, expectations, and assumptions are the downfall of our existence.

I love the gift of life, but do I sabotage it—consciously or not?

Each day is a gift, so why do we create misery on repeat?

There is no reason to live if there is no joy—no self-contentment.

We tend to prefabricate a joyless, unwanted, overly organised life.

Why?

Maybe it's the generational emotional cycle.

Maybe it's the need to dance with our emotional misery.

Maybe it's the fear of becoming a mere observer of life,

The fear of losing our carefully crafted identity.

If we take the sacred less seriously,

Then it no longer matters how we project ourselves to the world.

We begin to value the experience—without the self-imposed burdens.

Is that the way to embrace our universal mission?

Our Holy Spirit?

Perhaps it's just a matter of letting go,

Of unlearning what we've learnt,

Confessing our limitations, fears, and sorrows.

As a willing participant, I'm ready to reset myself—

To levitate into my life.

Can I reset myself?

Tough questions.

Have I simply evolved according to the commitments

Dictated by my self-awareness?

My walk back to the Airbnb is blessed with garden beds of snowdrops and jonquils—a sign of the coming spring.

My thoughts turn to my wife. I can see her on her knees, camera in hand, macro lens in place, capturing the hidden wonders within these botanical creatures.

She let me roam the world, knowing I'm searching for a deeper understanding of myself.

It takes courage and faith to let me go, especially knowing my mental health isn't always at its best.

She knows that being back here isn't a holiday.

I don't invite her to join the dance floor of my life story, but simply to be an observer of an uneasy evolution—a safe space for confidence.

If love means accepting another's weaknesses, then I truly believe I have the best lover in the world.

She is in my heart—Travelling without moving.

I added a photo of the snowdrops and jonquils to the family WhatsApp chat.

"I love you" were my words.

Chapter 15

I See The Trueness Of Life

In Ostend, my routine is to roam around like a tourist. Coffee shops, restaurants, a bit of cycling, and a fair dose of Thérèse. And when my head has gathered enough new insights about life and its universal mysteries, I retreat to the library to process and edit my novelistic work—shaping new understandings of life, my life, and the lives of future generations. That's my contribution to a better world.

Writing takes a lot of mental energy and fuel. I eat out of habit. I feel better when fasting, but eating is a good opportunity to observe and interact with the world. Wherever I go, there's always someone who tries to strike up a conversation with me.

I'm a magnet for free cheer-ups. A dispenser of wisdom. A Google Map on legs.

The interaction works both ways.

It cheers me up too. And newly acquired wisdom is worth its weight in gold.

I'm not invisible anymore. And I don't try to hide either.

At lunch, I watched a man chew for twenty-two minutes.

Not because I wanted to.

Because I couldn't stop noticing.

He sat across from me in a small restaurant near the promenade—blue K-Way jacket, patchy beard, the kind of sadness that doesn't announce itself but leaks out in posture. He ordered a burger and chips, unwrapped the serviette with military precision, and chewed each bite like it was a task assigned to him, not a choice.

I should've looked away.

But this is the curse of being observant.

I've got eagle eyes. I really do.

I notice everything. Always have.

The slight tremble in someone's hand when they pay with coins. The way a couple eats in silence, their knives clinking just a little too sharply. The waitress who smiles with her mouth but not her eyebrows.

Monitoring my spatial awareness is a form of survival.

It's exhausting.

That's what living through domestic violence does to you.

Always on alert for the unknown.

I see the fight two tables over—the one that's not loud but loaded. The glances. The fork jabbed a little too hard into a salad. I know they'll leave separately. I know she'll cry on the tram.

I see the old man who rearranges his cup three times before taking a sip. A ritual. A tic. Maybe a memory of a wife who used to bring it just so.

I see the barista who wipes the counter twice when no one's watching—not because it's dirty, but because she needs something to do with her hands before the panic returns.

I see it all.

And I can't unsee it.

I see the trueness of life.

It's not a gift. It's a frequency I can't tune out.

Back home, it made me good at work—reading rooms, catching silences, knowing when people were bluffing, or when a colleague was on the edge of a breakdown.

But it made friendships hard. Intimacy harder.

I'd see the lie before it was spoken.

I'd catch the hesitation in a compliment.

I'd sense the withdrawal before it arrived—and then couldn't pretend I hadn't.

People say they want to be seen.

But not like that.

Not with the lights on.

In Ostend, I thought I might switch it off. Be just another tourist. Take blurry photos of sunsets. Eat frites with mayo. Blend in.

But no.

Here I am, counting the minutes a stranger chews.

Feeling the ache in people I'll never speak to.

As a novelist, there's an upside. Good characters are born from observation and introspection. Anyone who has entered or exited my life has left an indelible footprint—something that can be transformed into the magical and meaningful.

Coco, Jay, Gaston, Ludo, Lucy—and so many others—didn't come from nowhere.

I should light a candle.

Not for the people I observe but for the part of me that keeps watching, even when it hurts.

Chapter 16

Was That A Prayer?

She walked in like she owned the place.

Tiny. Fierce. Wrapped in a thick floral scarf that looked like it had been through more winters than most marriages.

She carried a handbag the size of a carry-on and walked with a limp that said, "Don't you dare feel sorry for me."

She went straight to the candle stand, dug around in her bag for coins—which took a full minute—before finally dropping a five-euro note with the precision of someone paying off a debt.

Then she lit a big candle, stared up at Mary, and said—not whispered, said—"If you see my husband, tell him he still owes me money."

I nearly choked.

The other visitors shuffled uncomfortably, pretending not to hear her. I didn't even try to hide my grin.

Thérèse, of course, was thrilled.

"Finally, someone who's not afraid to pray with a little bite."

The widow stood there—legs apart, arms crossed—muttering what sounded like a running commentary on her late husband's shortcomings and discoloured personality.

"Three years he's been gone, and I'm still finding his dirty socks under the bed. If he's in heaven, they'd better show him where the laundry baskets are."

She lit a second candle—no extra donation—and added, "Tell him I said thank you, though. For the wine. He hated me drinking from his curated cellar."

The flame flickered violently for a moment.

She looked up at the statue of Mary like it owed her an explanation, then sighed and said, "Fine. I forgive him. Not for dying first."

Then she nodded—at Mary, at her memory, at the air—and walked out, dragging her feet across the stone floor like she was leaving a courtroom.

The scent of her perfume lingered behind: something between myrrh and neroli.

I turned to Thérèse. "Was that a prayer?"

"That," she said, "was a masterpiece."

I thought about it for a while.

How grief turns into humour. How anger finds strange resting places.

How faith sometimes sounds like talking back to ghosts.

Before I left, I lit a candle. Just one.

In memory of my paternal grandparents—Fernande and Nicolas—whom we weren't allowed to mix with when we were young.

Chapter 17

Alive

I prefer empty churches and holy intimacy.

I had no choice—Mass was on.

Seated in front of Thérèse, ready for my levitation ritual, I got the hiccups.

Not the whispery, ignorable kind. The loud, unpredictable kind that makes children giggle and pensioners turn around in disgust.

It started just as the organ began—a low G chord, a rise in harmony, an array of deep, resonant frequencies, and then—hic—me.

People were polite at first. I buried my face in my elbow. Held my breath. Swallowed hard. Tried to sit very still, as if that would stop my diaphragm from betraying me again.

It didn't.

The second one came mid-verse.

I sounded like a startled duck in a Walt Disney cartoon.

A man two pews up turned his head. The woman beside me offered a mint without making eye contact.

By the third hiccup, I knew I had to leave. But I didn't.

I don't know why.

Maybe because the sound of the choir made me forget I was embarrassed.

Or maybe because, somewhere deep in my chest, beneath the shame, I was laughing.

Not out loud—but inside.

Something had cracked open, and it wasn't just my breath.

It reminded me of the day the priest slapped me in the face for ringing the tiny church bells with too much conviction.

If he hadn't slapped me, I think the church's informal choir would have been his next target.

It sounded bad. Truly bad.

Half the boys mimed. The girls sang their hearts out—off-key.

Through the chaos, I was genuinely amused.

Shaking the bells freestyle was my way of contributing to the holy chaos.

I loved it.

Because I was finally part of something.

Inclusion is a human necessity—at least for me.

That feeling that God might notice you more if you stood up front and tried a little harder.

Eventually, the hiccups stopped—just in time for the final blessing.

I stayed until the end. Pretended I belonged.

Afterwards, an old woman—at least ninety, with bright red lipstick and a cane that looked like it had seen war—leaned in and said,

"You sounded alive, dear."

Alive.

Not disruptive. Not inappropriate.

Alive.

I smiled at God's little messenger.

I couldn't stop smiling.

All day, I smiled at my former self—the eleven-year-old choir boy—teasing the holy protocol.

I smiled to be alive.

Alive, I smiled.

I am alive—indeed, well alive.

Chapter 18

Some Prayers Are Drawn

He came in holding his mum's hand.

Couldn't have been older than six, maybe seven. Big eyes. Bigger silence.

His mum had that tired look parents carry when hope has been stretched too thin. She guided him to the candle rack like they'd done it before. Familiar but fragile.

She knelt down and whispered something in his ear. He nodded. Didn't speak.

He reached up, carefully, and placed a single coin into the box like he was defusing a bomb. She helped him light the candle. He didn't flinch at the flame.

Then he stood, hands folded in front of him, and stared

up at Mary.

No whisper. No prayer. Just... watching. Like he was waiting for her to blink.

He stayed like that for what felt like ten minutes. Didn't move. Didn't fidget. Just stared.

And Mary? For once, I swear she looked like she was listening.

The boy reached into his jacket pocket and pulled out a napkin. On it, in crayon, was a single red rose—lopsided, bright, blooming.

He walked forward, placed the napkin under the candle stand, and walked back. Still silent.

Then he gave his mum a nod. Not the kind that says "Let's go," but the kind that says, "I did it."

She smiled like she'd been holding her breath for years and could finally exhale.

As they turned to leave, he glanced at me. Just a flicker. Then gone.

Thérèse whispered, "Not all prayers need sound. Some are drawn."

The boy never spoke a word. But when the doors closed behind them, the whole church felt like it had heard something.

I walked up, looked at the napkin. The rose was simple, a little messy. But it had heart.

I left it there. Didn't touch it. Just lit a candle next to his, closed my eyes, and listened.

Silence can be deafening and sacred.

As I was ready to take notes on my phone, I came across one of my manual transcript journal entries dated 2006. It reads:

He leaned on his crutches—thin aluminium sticks that clicked with each motion. Each step cost him. Not in pain, but in breath. In will. He took it slowly. The air inside the church was cooler than outside—touched by the scent of frankincense, candle smoke, and the faint must of age-old stone. But to him, it smelled of memory. Of solemn places. Of beginnings that never blossomed.

His hair, sparse and silver, was combed with care, and he wore a light grey jacket over a woollen jumper—chosen more for dignity than for warmth. He was a Chinese national, touring Europe with friends and family. The group had stopped here on the itinerary: "Ostend – St Peter and St Paul Church. 45 minutes." Most of the other visitors had gone toward the nave, chattering softly in Mandarin and Cantonese, phones clicking. But he turned left.

Left, toward the alcove of Mary.

He dragged himself along the pews, the crutches tapping a quiet rhythm against the polished floor. A few heads turned, then turned away. He was used to it. There had been a time when he would've bowed in embarrassment, made himself smaller. But not anymore. Not now, on the last journey of his life.

The music of the organ filled the space—deep, rolling chords that echoed like old thunder beneath the vaulted ceiling. A young man played at the altar, unaware—or unconcerned—by the foreign elder limping across the chapel, who slowly welcomed the music that drowned out his laboured breath and made his entrance feel like something sacred.

And there she was—Mary.

The mosaic was luminous even in shadow. White abaculi shaped her face with impossible softness, her eyes cast downward in infinite patience. Her hands reached forward—not out, but down—as if inviting what had fallen to rise. To try again.

The senior traveller paused before the black steel candle stand. He stood still, wheezing gently. His left crutch trembled in place. His free hand reached slowly into the pocket of his coat. An army of coins was always there, always prepared. It had become a ritual on this tour. Antwerp. Brussels. Bruges. Now Ostend. And after this? Ghent.

Each church felt different.

He inserted the coin gently, as if not to disturb the silence, and selected a white candle. His fingers moved with reverence, his entire body shifting to balance against the crutches. He used an already-lit flame to catch his wick. It took at once. A clean, hopeful glow.

He bowed his head slightly—not in Christian faith, but in something else. Cultural respect. A nod to every altar he had ever walked past, every prayer he had never dared to speak aloud.

He sat slowly on the nearby pew, the candle flickering in his periphery. His breath had still not returned, but he didn't care. His eyes were fixed on Mary.

The bitterness inside him was quiet. But it was there. Loudly quiet.

He rested his hand on his knee. The skin was paper-thin now. The veins shone through like roads on a faded map.

He did not cry. It looked like that part of him had been emptied years ago. But his face was taut, every muscle frozen in concentration, as if by staring long enough, Mary might speak. Might say: You are forgiven, even though you never asked.

He spoke quietly. The words were Mandarin. Slow. Barely above a whisper.

I thought I had more time, was the translation of his facial expression.

He fell silent.

The organist paused, perhaps sensing the atmosphere shift. The cathedral, for a fleeting moment, held its breath with him.

Then he stood.

It took time. He pushed himself up with both crutches. He looked once more at Mary—not pleading now, but offering a soft, weary nod. Not of thanks. Not of farewell. Just an acceptance.

He walked the aisle in reverse, each step slower than the last. His breath wheezed but stayed steady. A man moving forward—if only toward the exit.

Chapter 19

The Wrong Shoes

He fell at the tram stop.

No drama. No thud that made people gasp. Just a slow, sideways collapse—like a tree leaning into the inevitable.

I was five steps behind him, sipping from my water bottle and minding my own business. Then I was beside him, kneeling, hands unsure where to land.

"Are you alright?" I asked.

He looked up at me with the dull surprise of someone who hadn't expected to still be alive.

"Bit of a slip," he muttered.

He wasn't hurt—not really. A scuffed palm, pride in pieces. I helped him sit on the bench. Offered water—He refused.

Dusted himself off.

And that's when I saw it.

His shoes didn't match.

Both black, yes. Both leather. But one was a loafer—smooth and rounded. The other, a boot—sturdy, laced, made for colder weather.

The sort of mismatch that doesn't happen unless something else is slipping.

He caught me looking.

"They look the same from a distance," he said, not unkindly.

I smiled. I didn't respond. Just nodded, like mismatched shoes were the latest trend.

We sat there a few minutes more. He didn't ask my name. I didn't ask his story.

But when the tram arrived, I helped him up again. He boarded with a grunt and a wave.

I stood there a long time after he left. Not because I was shaken, but because I couldn't stop thinking about the shoes.

How long had it taken him to notice? Did he even care? Had someone else noticed first?

I thought about all the days I'd walked around with something wrong and no one had said a word.

Sadness tucked under my collar. Regret stuffed in my pockets.
A tiredness I wore like cologne.

I wear my mistakes like clothes sometimes.

Not sometimes—often.

And people let me.

They don't care. They're too busy wearing their own.

My thoughts aren't as dark as my brother's.

But sometimes, everything is grey.

This is why I come to Ostend.

To blend my greyness into the greyness of the North Sea
and its greyish skies.

Ostend and Thérèse are the anchors of my renaissance.

TWO EURO CANDLES

Chapter 20

Not A Drive-Thru

"You're all doing it wrong," Thérèse said one morning, out of nowhere.

I was halfway through sending a message, sitting in my usual pew, watching a lady light a candle while FaceTiming someone in California.

"I beg your pardon?" I said, trying not to drop my phone.

"Prayer. Candles. This whole wish-list-to-heaven business. It's not a drive-thru."

I raised an eyebrow. "Tell that to the bloke who asked for better Wi-Fi yesterday."

"Exactly," she snapped. "Miracles aren't express shipping. They're more like compost. You bury something deep, leave it in the dark, and wait."

"Wait for what?"

"For it to rot into something useful. Without questioning the process."

That shut me up.

Not only did it shut me up, but harpooned me deep inside.

I never bury things. Everything is well and truly alive in my mental carousel. In all the cells of my body.

The good. The bad. The ugly.

I couldn't bury my pain.

Just as Mary keeps a ledger for candle donations, I keep a pain ledger.

It's full, alive, and reeks like rotten compost—but it's authentic in its rawness.

Strangers would be horrified if the contents of my ledger ever came to light.

I'm not here to hurt anyone—I'm here for peace. Clarity.

Maybe Thérèse is right. Maybe it's time to bury things.

Useless past. Emotional triggers. Hurts. Grief. Family hooks.

Thérèse was on a roll now. "People think faith is about outcomes. But it's really about attention. About how willing you are to look at the same thing again and again until you see it properly."

I watched a man light two candles, kneel, and then immediately start checking his smartwatch.

Thérèse groaned. "If I had a dollar for every time someone tried to outsource their spiritual work—well, I'd still be a nun. But I'd be a smug one."

I laughed. "So what's the 'right' way, then? Should I dig a big hole on the beach to bury my burden?"

"There's no formula—that's the point. Be honest. Be small. Be bothered enough to keep showing up, even when it's boring. Especially when it's boring."

"It isn't boring. It's immensely hurtful."

Thérèse giggled. "Your approach is boring and hurtful. Stop hurting yourself. Simply confess your burdens and the Holy Spirit will take care of everything. It'll bury, dilute, and recycle whatever you feel or experience into holy blessings."

That shut me up again.

I'd never imagined God running an emotional compost yard—though He probably invented it as part of His holy creation.

Thérèse murmured, "God gave everyone the right life experiences to experience. It's our choice how we deal with them. Making a mountain out of them was your choice. Making a fountain of youth out of them would've been a better one. God never ages. We do—by choice. We kill ourselves slowly."

"You mean humans can achieve eternity?"

"Yes. Not by dancing around or over-analysing their failed life experiences. Humans are creators—as much as God is. So just create."

"You mean creating a purposeful life can guide you toward eternity? What about you?"

"I've been well and truly alive since 1873, and I'm not ready to separate myself from the love of God."

"I didn't mean to be rude or diminish you in any way. I like your answer."

"Maxsense, I've seen you every year since you were a kid, trying to comprehend yourself. There is nothing wrong with you. And there never was. Please confess your burdens to God and let your Creator take over."

"Confess and create. That's how miracles work!"

"Every time you run away, you separate yourself from the love of God."

That shut me up again—for the third time.

A man sneezed and it echoed like a gunshot through the church. Ceramic Mary wasn't fazed. I silently thanked him for the distraction.

"The sacred is in the repetition," Thérèse added. "Not the reward."

"Starting with confession, right?" I said loudly.

I looked around the church. Same stained-glass windows. Same rows of flickering candles. Same woman whispering to Mary like she was calling in a favour.

And yet… it didn't feel the same. Not now.

"Also," Thérèse added, "stop asking for parking spots. That's not an act of creation."

"Guilty," I muttered.

"Next time, ask for patience. Then get stuck in traffic. That's how it works."

She was half-joking. I think.

Before I left, I lit a candle—not for anything in particular. Just to celebrate something new that I can't yet comprehend. It burned slowly. Quietly. Like something learning how to begin.

TWO EURO CANDLES

Chapter 21

I Didn't Know What To Say

She was sitting on a bench near the seafront, eyes red, tissues balled in her lap like used confessions. She wasn't sobbing, just leaking. Quietly. The kind of sadness that no longer needs to explain itself.

I saw her as I passed, slowed my pace, then stopped just beyond the bench, like I'd suddenly forgotten where I was going.

I looked back. She saw me. She was homeless.

And for the smallest second, she looked like she was hoping I might say something.

But I didn't.

I smiled politely—tight-lipped, apologetic—and kept walking.

It took me twenty minutes to get back to the flat, but I never really left that bench.

I boiled water for tea. Forgot the bag. Stared at the kettle like it might forgive me.

I kept seeing her face. Not just the tears, but the way her shoulders were trying to stay still. How her mouth had opened slightly, like the beginning of a word that never came.

I should've said something.

But what?

"Are you alright?"

Too generic.

"Do you want me to sit with you?"

Too bold.

"Can I get you something? A coffee? A blanket? A bit of silence that isn't yours alone? A bit of privacy?"

Too late.

I went back. Same bench. Same street kerb. Empty.

No trace of her. Just seagull droppings and a cigarette butt crushed near the leg. I sat down and stared at the sea until it blurred.

In my phone, I wrote:

I didn't know what to say.

But maybe I didn't need to say anything.

Maybe she just needed someone not to walk away.

And I did.

I locked my phone and felt it—shame, quiet and heavy.

I know well the feeling of being broke, bankrupt, unable to pay the rent or even read the eviction notice.

I know the bitterness when the credit cards are blocked, and the bank overdrafts are stretched far beyond their limits.

The only thing left is you.

You and your shadow, sitting on benches.

Driving to nowhere in search of a band-aid solution.

Trying to fill my lungs, to swim against the tide with tired arms, in an attempt to protect and provide for the ones I love.

They're all that matter now.

Even through my fall from grace, it remained my responsibility to find a new roof, put food on the table, cover the basics of life—while hiding the pain of my reality from their eyes.

At night, my understanding was as dark as the sky.

I had worked hard all my life, only to accumulate debt.

I was the problem—my emotional shortcomings sabotaged me.

I ran away before I could reap the rewards of my work.

My core values couldn't tolerate the falseness, deception, or unethical nature of the deal that was being offered. There was big money to be made—but not at someone else's expense.

I turned away from the gold and the glitter.

My skills and talents were never the issue. I just let the wrong people into my life. Again and again.

I was thirsty for success.

Success at any cost. Maybe?

I was searching for a trampoline to launch me to success.

A trampoline to prove to my father I wasn't an idiot.

A trampoline that fed my cycles of anger, resentment, frustration.

I never had trouble finding a job or committing to one — until I realised it was draining me. The light of success never came; maybe it had never existed.

On autopilot, my inner greyness and darkness had already taken over.

There was no way back.

Another crash. Another fall.

My father was right.

I am an idiot.

Let me try another trampoline.

Life isn't short of trampolines.

I'm just running out of breath.

My arms and legs are sore.

My limbs are buckling—still, I'm standing.

The last man standing, as always.

Like an idiot.

An idiot who didn't get, or grasp, life's lessons.

Am I an idiot?

That's a tough question for me to answer.

Maybe it's a fifty-fifty.

I'm aware of my shortcomings—but am I aware enough?

Has learning so much about myself made me a better person?

I don't know. I doubt it sometimes.

Confusion is an intimate enemy.

Should I confess that too?

That afternoon, I lit a candle at the church.

Not for the homeless girl. Not exactly for me.

Thérèse didn't speak that day.

But I felt something soft settle around me.

A knowing.

A permission to try again.

So I made a vow—not out loud, not formal. Just inward:

> *No more bouncier trampolines.*
>
> *Just a slow ascension.*

Chapter 22

Polygamy And Prayer Candles

He walked in wearing leather shoes far too shiny for honesty and a camel coat that probably cost more than my rent back home. Hair slicked, watch polished, the air around him thick with male-designed fragrance and overconfidence.

Thérèse sniffed dramatically. "Oh goodie. A walking parable."

He strutted up to the candle rack and began lighting candles—one after the other. Six in total.

"Six. It must be serious," I muttered.

Then he bowed his head slightly and, without shame, said loudly, "One for each of them. Lord, help them be kind to me. Or at least stop messaging each other."

Thérèse let out the holiest of snorts. "I knew it. Polygamy

and prayer candles. A combination as old as time."

The man crossed himself with flair, then looked around to see who'd witnessed his macho devotion. I lowered my head, trying not to make eye contact.

"Do you reckon they all know about each other?" I whispered to Thérèse.

"They do now," she said. "Never underestimate women with data plans."

He turned to leave, pausing just long enough to drop another coin in the box. "And for the kids," he said. "All nine of them."

"Nine?" I blinked.

"Miracles, every one," he said proudly.

"Poor woman," said Thérèse.

"Which one?"

"All of them."

He strutted out the door like a man convinced his problems were now Mary's.

I sat back and watched the six flames flicker. One flared suddenly, then settled. The others danced quietly, each with its own rhythm.

I thought about what it meant to be prayed for by someone who'd likely disappointed you. What it meant to be included—

if only in wax.

"Is it still love," I asked, "if it's messy and misguided?"

"It's especially love if it's messy and misguided," Thérèse said. "The neat kind never makes it past the first real argument, or the first acknowledgement of our inbuilt differences."

"So, is accepting someone else's differences true love?" I asked.

Thérèse didn't reply.

Maybe she was too busy mending the lives of six wives and nine kids.

I didn't light a candle that day.

I lit nine of them—with my lunch money.

Let the kids speak their own truth.

TWO EURO CANDLES

Chapter 23

Stranger At My Table

The sun was out on Albert I Promenade.

Hundreds of tourists rushed to secure chairs and tables.

Lunch was soon.

The seagulls—each the size of a World War II bomber—were getting nervous.

She didn't ask.

Just sat down across from me, dropped a handbag onto the table, and unwrapped a pack of crisps like she'd been expected.

We were in a takeaway joint overlooking the North Sea—four tiny tables, an out-of-order Coke sign, and the faint smell of oil that never left your jacket.

I'd come in to hide from the wind and nurse a plate of stoofvlees.

"You don't mind, do you?" she asked, halfway through her filet américain sandwich.

I blinked. "No, go ahead."

She didn't thank me. Just opened a Fanta and started talking.

Her Irish accent brought something exotic to my day.

She talked about the dog she'd had as a kid.

About the ex who once broke up with her via Post-it note and a bottle of cheap champagne left in the fridge.

About the woman she was travelling with—"sweet, but a spiritual beige."

There were no filters in her stories. As authentic as it gets.

I nodded through mouthfuls, unsure if I'd been mistaken for someone else or simply chosen.

I attract this sort of thing.

Strangers like to strike up conversations with me.

It's fun, light-hearted—cheap wisdom on the go.

She was in her mid-thirties, maybe. Backpack on the floor. A face that carried tiredness well.

She spoke with the rhythm of someone used to filling silences before they had a chance to thicken.

I offered her some of my fries and stoofvlees.

She accepted like it was a sacrament.

She was definitely hungry. Or maybe she hadn't had a cooked meal in ages.

When I asked her name, she paused.

"Does it matter?" she said.

And somehow, it didn't.

We sat there for half an hour. Ate. Shared silence between stories.

Laughed once—not loud, but real.

Her voice was warm and authentic.

Simply Irish.

Then she stood, wiped her hands on a napkin, and said,

"Thanks for not making it weird."

She left before I could reply.

I looked down at her empty Fanta can.

It still had her lipstick mark on the rim.

I wrote:

> *Some people arrive without warning.*
> *Fill the space like they've been there before.*

Say exactly what you didn't know you needed to hear.

Then leave—like it was no big deal.

That night, I walked around the church but didn't go in.

It was closed.

I just stood across the road, watching the windows dark glow, like the pause of held breath.

My one-sixth romantic and one-sixth melancholic persona took over my headspace.

I imagined the Irish girl sitting at a candlelit table somewhere else in town, talking to another stranger.

And maybe that's all we are to each other, really.

Flickers in the story.

Uninvited graces.

Visitors who teach us how to stay present.

Even if it's just over one plate of chips and stoofvlees.

And bang.

The penny dropped.

She was a living image of Abigail Ashton, one of the six women featured in my previous novel.

This time around she had no visible disabilities and no black eyes—just careless warmth and authenticity.

Miracles happen.

Maybe she was God's messenger, inviting me to continue with the second and third instalments of Jay Smith's trilogy.

Something deep inside is telling me to follow through.

Something that doesn't require candles.

Just the call to create—In the holy literary garden.

TWO EURO CANDLES

Chapter 24

Young Faith

She walked in as if she wasn't sure she was allowed.

Barely sixteen. Hair tied back into a knot that was more practical than stylish. She smelled faintly of the North Sea—salt, fish scales, and a hint of teenage rebellion.

Thérèse whispered, "She's one of mine."

The girl made a beeline for the candle stand, dug a couple of euros out of her hoodie pocket, and paused. She looked up at Mary like she was making a deal with the holy CEO's representative.

"Please," she whispered. "Just make my skin clear up before Saturday night."

I blinked. That was it.

She lit the candle. Watched it burn for a moment. Then added, "And maybe make Joris notice I exist. But mainly the skin."

Thérèse sighed, soft and fond. "Oh, that kind of prayer still works."

The girl stood there a little longer. No tears. No theatrics. Just that quiet, urgent kind of hope only teenagers seem to master. Then she walked out, head up, steps light.

"Do you reckon she'll get her miracle?" I asked.

"Not in the way she wants. But yes."

"Young faith," Thérèse added. "It's loud and awkward, but it lights up the sky when it lands."

I looked at the candle she'd left behind. It burned with a sharp, steady flame. Like it had a point to prove.

I lit one beside hers, just for the sake of it. Not for acne. Not for Joris. Just for the right to want something simple, dumb, and beautiful.

We all deserve that much.

I wish I'd known that when I was a kid.

Outside the church, I saw her again—feeding chips to a seagull with one hand and texting furiously with the other. She laughed at something on her screen.

My stomach was screaming—lunchtime.

I couldn't resist its calling.

Ordering fish in a café that had three pasta specials on the board and only a handful of diners was a stupid decision. I was tired of bread and cheese, and the photo on the laminated menu—showing a sole meunière swimming in a brown butter sauce, surrounded by lemon slices and fresh parsley—found the right place in my mind, even if the picture looked like something out of Midjourney.

I should've known better.

The fish arrived still staring at me. Skin crisped, tail curled. A little too beautiful to trust.

I declined the waiter's offer to clean the sole for me. I'd done it plenty of times while working as a university student in a Chinese restaurant.

The fish looked well cooked and didn't carry any of the gingery, fragrant notes I'd come to associate with Asian cuisine.

My skilled woodworker's hands knew how to handle a fork and spoon, extracting the four fillets from the dorsal and anal fins with grace and precision.

The fish was delicious—and far better looking than the one on the laminated menu poster.

I made it halfway through before it happened.

A bone—tiny, sharp—lodged itself in the back of my throat.

First came the cough. Subtle. Dry.

Then a gulp of water.

Then a panic that bloomed fast and hot in my chest.

I tried not to make a scene. Kept sipping. Swallowed again. Another cough.

People turned.

I stood up, motioned to the waiter, and said in my best tourist-dignified wheeze:

"I... I..."

He didn't wait for the rest.

Next thing I knew, I was sitting on a plastic chair out the back near the kitchen, leaning forward while someone rubbed my back and whispered calm instructions in Dutch.

"Okay, Lieverd. We're going to fix this."

Her voice was soft, steady, reassuring.

She was maybe in her late fifties. Hair in a tight bun. Smelled faintly of eucalyptus—and whatever comfort sounds like in physical form. She tilted my head, held my chest and spine with both hands, handed me water, and asked me to cough again—this time properly.

I did. Twice.

She nodded. Calm as a nurse in an emergency ward.

I coughed again.

Third time lucky.

The bone dislodged.

I burst into tears.

Not loud ones. Just the quiet, shameful trickle of someone who's been holding too much, for too long, and finally cracked in the most ridiculous setting possible.

"I'm sorry," I said.

She smiled. "Never apologise for being scared."

I don't remember what happened next. Somehow, I ended up back at my table. The fish had been cleared. A dessert had appeared—a slice of apple tart, on the house.

I didn't ask questions.

I ate it slowly. Carefully. Gratefully.

I paid. I left a generous tip.

Back on the street, her scent lingered—but not as much as her words.

"Never apologise for being scared" has been added to my confession list.

TWO EURO CANDLES

Chapter 25

You're Not Here By Accident

I came in late that day, half-wet from the rain and in a foul mood. My coffee had spilled on my coat, my phone and wallet were soggy, and I'd forgotten why I even bothered anymore.

The church was quieter than usual—just me, a cleaner dusting a side altar, and a young bloke taking blurry photos of everything on his phone.

I used to take blurry photos too. The light inside the church isn't always kind to photographers. Sometimes it's muted and domed; other times, too heavenly—too powerful.

I sat down, dropped my jacket with a wet plop, and sighed so loudly it echoed.

"That dramatic exhale was a bit much," said Thérèse.

I didn't answer.

"You think you're just here to watch," she continued. "To scribble and judge and shake your clever little head. But you were brought here."

"By what, divine GPS?"

"Don't flatter yourself," she said. "More like a long series of tiny nudges: that missed train, that cancelled job, the anti-corruption enquiry, that café that gave you the wrong order but the right seat by the window. And today, the rain."

I paused. She wasn't wrong.

"Even the pigeons were in on it," she added.

I let out a small laugh. "You're telling me my entire life has been one long breadcrumb trail to this church?"

"Yes," she said. "But you only noticed the crumbs once you sat still."

I looked around. Same candles, same statue, same dusty smell. But today, with her words, it felt… precise. Like someone had been setting this moment up for a while.

A man walked past me and muttered a prayer about his daughter coming home. A kid giggled as her dad lit a candle too slowly. A woman entered crying and left humming.

It wasn't random. None of it.

"I don't believe in fate," I said.

"Good," said Thérèse. "This isn't fate. This is invitation."

I sat there, unsure whether to laugh or light something.

In the end, I did both.

It was the bubble of oxygen my head needed.

I felt radiant and warm in a place that suddenly felt very good.

My glow was as bright as the radiant rack of candles.

And then she appeared.

An Indian lady dressed in traditional clothing in a Catholic church.

I didn't expect that.

Had her naan-crumb trail guided her inside?

The light and atmosphere inside the church turned, almost naturally, into a Bollywood production—in a very humble and respectful way.

It was an unreal cinematic scene, and I couldn't help but capture it on my phone.

> *The doors shut gently behind her, sealing her away from the North Sea wind. A shiver traced the length of her spine, even beneath the layers of her pashmina shawl. The sudden stillness felt like an intake of breath—sacred and immense. The scent of centuries pressed into her lungs. She stood still just past the entry, her slippers silent against the floor, her eyes adjusting to the golden gloom.*

Above her, light poured through the stained-glass windows in fractured glory—jewel-toned reflections dancing across the nave, making the space breathe in shifting hues of ruby, sapphire, emerald. It fell on statues and saints, on worn pews and forgotten leaflets, and now on her face—brown and tear-marked. She did not wipe them. Not yet.

She moved gently, as if her presence might disturb the spirits here. She wore a long rust-orange kurta under the warmth of her earthy woollen wrap, her dark hair bound in a simple braid, with oil still clinging faintly to its length. Her bangles, thinned by wear, rubbed with the softest chime as she walked. Her feet, wrapped in socks and slippers more suited to temple floors than the Belgian chill, made no sound.

To her left, Mary awaited.

The white mosaic shimmered under the soft, dispersed light. Mary was caught mid-embrace—open arms, sorrowful eyes, head tilted in still mercy. Her presence struck the woman not with familiarity, but with grace. Foreign, yes. But not unkind.

She approached the black steel candle stand with reverence, each step a quiet plea. She stopped before it and stood still. Her breath shook in her chest. She reached into her pocket—a cloth-lined one, sewn discreetly into the side of her kurta—and retrieved a single coin. It had been prepared for this moment.

The coin clinked into the slot with an echo that felt too loud, too final. She selected a candle, its white wax smooth under her fingertips. Lighting it took time. The wick hesitated. Her hands were not steady. Her kurta sleeves were in the way. She repositioned herself with grace, held the candle with a firmer hand, and on the third strike, the flame bloomed into a steady glow.

She set the candle into place, inhaled, and exhaled slowly, fingers brushing her lips and then her forehead in an improvised gesture of respect. Her body bent forward slightly—not in a curtsy or bow, but in the deep-set cultural rhythm of offering. Not to Mary. Not exactly. But to something beyond.

Then she stepped to the pew closest to the mural and sat.

The wooden bench was cold beneath her, a contrast to the inner fire twisting in her belly. Her palms pressed together in prayer—not quite Hindu, not quite Catholic—a fusion of learned grace and ancestral reflex. She gazed at Mary as one might gaze at a stranger in a crowd who suddenly smiles and makes you feel known.

She let her tears fall silently. They were not theatrical. They were not performed. They were salt and release—tiny rivers down cheeks already carved by long days and longer questions. She asked for no miracle. Only understanding. Only peace.

Her fingers played with the gold thread at the end of her shawl, tugging gently—a nervous tic from girlhood days. Outside, the grey sky pressed close to the city. Four degrees—cold enough to chill the bones—but inside this space, warmth filtered not through heat, but through light. The light of the stained glass now washed the mosaic in hues of lavender and rose, softening Mary's gaze even more.

She stayed seated for a long time, hands folded in her lap, body still. Her breath slowed. Her spine, once curled, straightened slightly. There was no answer from above. No voice. No wind.

Only the flicker of her candle. The hush of the church. The fading scent of something sweet in the air.

Eventually, she stood. Her legs ached slightly from the cold bench, but she moved with poise. She glanced once more at Mary, bowed her head—not in worship, but in mutual understanding—and turned.

She walked back through the same aisle, retracing her steps as the light shifted across her path. Her braid swung gently between her shoulder blades, and her shawl trailed behind her like a curtain of rust and gold. She didn't wipe her tears now—they had dried. Her eyes were red, yes—but calm.

Chapter 26

The Towel Smells Like Her

It wasn't immediate.

I stepped out of the shower, wrapped the towel around my shoulders, rubbed my face into the fabric—and there it was.

Musky jasmine and clean cotton.

The ghost of a scent I hadn't noticed in years.

It smelled like her.

Not exactly. Not like her skin, or her hair, or her perfume. But like her presence—that impossible-to-bottle blend of softness, sandalwood soap, and the kind of laundry detergent she insisted on using, even though it cost more and gave her mild skin allergies.

I stood there dripping onto the tiled floor, heart thumping

like I'd just been caught.

It had been over thirty years.

We broke up in spring, on a Wednesday. It was dramatic. Just two people in a too-small apartment realising that love is not the same thing as staying.

She didn't just scream. She threw things.

A lot of things. Not just my things.

Everything.

Oranges, high ceilings and rage were a bad combo.

Our reactive behaviours came to a head.

One more time.

We'd already broken up three times, but this time, we were living together.

We weren't strangers.

We were supposed to be lovers.

Whatever.

It didn't happen.

We weren't bad people.

We just didn't see the big picture.

We didn't know how to communicate our fears, traumas and hurts.

We never approached the core of our cores.

We were defensive. Protective. Tired and in love.

The wrong kind of love.

The kind that hurts even when you say, "I love you."

She was smart, beautiful, had a great laugh—and a few emotional triggers that could end love in seconds.

I wasn't any better. I was already a runaway boy, ready to run again.

Her need for control was a trap for me.

My need for freedom was her fear.

Looking back, we were stupid or naive.

Emotionally ignorant.

The ugly build-up to the breakup had made its way under our roof.

Within weeks, I ended up with bruised blue ears and a stranger in our bed.

Anger and I were one.

It became a hurtful ping-pong game of betrayal.

An endless escalation of poor human emotions.

Poor human conditioning.

I packed my things, and I didn't go back for the little bits that make love stick together.

I didn't go back for the crystal glasses engraved with our names.

Our first holiday photos.

My record collection—the one that made her dance and smile all night.

I didn't go back for that.

I did go back though, only once, and by invitation.

Her mum, fearing for her daughter's wellbeing, had asked me to sort things out.

I went.

That was a mistake.

When she opened the door, the only thing visible was her breast.

Not the one I knew.

Her hormones had gone wild since our breakup. Within weeks, her chest had seemed to triple in size, and she used that sudden change as a lure to bring me back home.

She failed.

I wasn't interested.

Sex without love wasn't for me.

Feeling rejected, her words of war blasted into the street.

She became mad and physical.

I avoided a hard punch to the face by pushing her.

A bad move—an instant regret.

Her head knocked hard against the door.

That was the end.

The real end.

That day, I felt small.

I was like my father—a wife-basher.

An arsehole.

For over twenty years, I carried that picture in my head.

That sensation in my heart.

It consumed me. Badly.

A few years ago, I travelled to Belgium and met her.

I apologised before any kind of conversation.

It was sincere.

Not a one-way apology to make myself feel better.

I offered an apology to honour her—and the life we had shared.

To my surprise, she didn't remember a thing.

She didn't remember the incident—our final breakup.

She simply remembered that she was in love with me.

That's what she confessed to her therapist.

I didn't entertain the subject.

My therapists also knew that she was more than love.

In the days after our reunion, I didn't feel particularly good.

I was shocked. Humbled. Quiet. And stupid.

How was it possible that she didn't remember the most traumatic day of our life together?

I was speechless.

Saddened, somehow. Truly shocked.

My apology triggered something deep and unsettled in her.

She reached out.

She didn't mince her words.

She was back in total war mode.

Her feelings of rejection were still alive—burning since the day she tried to bring me back home.

With great innocence, my apology rekindled the fire of our individual and shared emotional poverty.

It hurt, but my inner observer told me there was nothing I could do.

The fire would burn itself out, somehow.

And now, in a tiny flat in Ostend, wrapped in a stranger's towel, I decided to observe only the sweetest part of our union.

The Sunday mornings in bed.

Bertignac et les Visiteurs.

The red glossy skirting board.

The kitchen wallpaper.

The Renault 5.

I didn't cry.

But something inside me wilted, gently.

Like a flower that finally stopped holding its breath.

I sat on the edge of the bed, towel around my shoulders, and whispered her name like another small apology.

It didn't echo.

But it didn't disappear either.

Later that day, I lit a candle.

For her. For me.

For what we couldn't grow.

For what we did, once, with the little light we had.

And later, as I dried my hands on that same towel, I smiled.

Maybe grief is just love that's learned to wait.

Chapter 27

Pilgrims Without Luggage

They came in like a gust of wind—loud, chatty, hiking shoes squeaking on the old polished floor. A tour group. Ages somewhere between seventy and confused. Lanyards, laminated name tags, sun hats in March. The works.

I watched them spill into the church like schoolkids on an excursion, all elbows—and elbows again. One woman gasped at the ceiling. Another tried to bring a pigeon inside.

Thérèse sighed. "Bless them. They came for the architecture, but they might leave with something better."

"Architecture was my initial motive too," I replied softly.

Thérèse giggled. "I stopped counting how many times you took pictures of me. I felt like a supermodel."

"You're a part of me that I can't take photos of," I murmured, looking Thérèse gently in the eyes.

The tourists circled the statue of Mary, taking turns with their cameras and candle selfies. A man in cargo pants whispered, "Do we pay before or after the miracle?"

Someone giggled. Someone else lit a candle and prayed out loud: "World peace, less arthritis, and if possible, a good Belgian beer later."

And yet—among the bustle, something strange happened.

One woman, maybe mid-sixties, stayed behind while the group moved on. She wasn't wearing a lanyard. No camera. Just stood there, eyes glassy, hands clutched together like she was holding back a scream—or a memory.

Her physical body mirrored her stiff emotional baggage.

She knelt, slowly, and rested her forehead against the iron base of the candle stand.

The chatter faded. Even the organ rehearsal paused.

She whispered something I couldn't hear, then stayed like that. Still. Vulnerable. Unashamed.

Thérèse whispered, "There's always one."

When she finally stood up, she looked taller. Not physically—spiritually. Like she'd left something behind and it had made space in her.

"Where did her trauma go? Where is her pain?" I asked Thérèse. She did not answer.

The lady rejoined the group without a word. Someone passed her a water bottle. She smiled and said thank you.

That's all. The atmosphere in front of Mary was lighter and warmer.

The rest of the group took turns lighting candles—some laughing, some serious, some just curious. Then they gathered near the exit, already talking about where to get waffles.

But the stillness lingered.

"They didn't carry much," I said. "No real luggage."

"Maybe," said Thérèse, "but the best pilgrims never do."

"What about the weight on their shoulders?" I queried.

"Humans are the only ones seeing the weights and the baggage. Mary and I only see God's creation—as perfect as they come."

Thérèse's answer kept me quiet for a while.

I stayed a little longer, watching their candles burn. Some flickered wildly. One went out. One burned blue.

Before I left, I lit a candle for the quiet woman. For the thing she didn't say. For the thing I didn't say. And for everyone who wanders in thinking it's just a bus stop on the map, only to realise they've just arrived—within.

"Will I ever arrive?" I asked Mary.

"There are no destinations in God's creation. Always love. Always motion," whispered Thérèse.

In Ostend, my reactive behaviours and anxiety were like a simmering sauce evaporating quietly on the hot stove's back burner.

Maybe my brother, the one in my dream, was right. I am getting softer, gentler, and in love with myself.

Chapter 28

On Their Bloody Phone

I was sitting in a café that had the audacity to play jazz at 9 a.m.

Real jazz, too—brassy, unpredictable, full of notes that didn't want to be caught. My coffee was decent, the croissant was okay, and everyone around me was… gone.

Not physically. They were there.

But not there.

One table over, a couple sat in total silence, their thumbs dancing like they were in separate auditions. He scrolled. She scrolled. Their drinks sweated on the table between them, untouched. I stared longer than I should've. No eye contact. No smiles. No words.

Across the room, a girl in her twenties took fifteen selfies in three poses, checked them, frowned, and deleted them all. Then started again.

Next to me, a toddler tried to hand his mother a piece of biscuit. She didn't look up.

Suddenly, everything I'd come to Ostend to escape was right here in this little jazz-lit room:

Distraction. Disconnection. Despair. All in high definition.

I wanted to scream: "Look up! You're here! You're alive! You've been given breath and chocolates and conversations waiting to happen—and you're watching a reel of someone else's breakfast!"

But I didn't.

I just finished my latte and left.

And as I walked, I realised—I was guilty too.

I'd been checking the news and my emails four times a day. I'd posted a photo of the North Sea with a vaguely meaningful caption. I'd left WhatsApp unread just so I wouldn't have to engage.

Because presence is harder than performance.

I found myself in front of the train station. Sat on a bench. Watched real pigeons doing their pigeon thing. Watched people walk by.

And then—I put my phone away.

Properly away.

Not in my hand. Not in my lap.

Gone.

At first, I felt naked. Disarmed. Like someone had taken away a limb that I only remembered I had when it buzzed.

But then I breathed.

And I noticed the way the light fell on the statues near the entry.

And the sound of two old women arguing in West Flemish about tarts.

And the laughter of a teenager so joyful I nearly cried.

And a child waving at the world just to see who would wave back.

I did.

And she smiled.

I don't know what changed after that. But something softened. A little bit more.

Maybe it's my melancholy, and my romanticism tinting my vision with the colour of love.

That afternoon, at the church, I didn't take a photo of the candle I lit. I just watched it burn. Listened to its flicker.

Said a quiet prayer for everyone hunched over their screens, chasing meaning in pixels.

And one for me.

That I'd remember how to look up.

And not miss my own life.

I turned to Thérèse.

Without filters, peace and beauty were her.

I wish I could say the same about me.

Then, I remembered Thérèse's word.

I am a creator.

Peace and beauty are within my reach.

Chapter 29

Something Is Beginning

The church felt different that day.

I couldn't explain it. The same stone floor, the same weak sunlight sneaking through stained glass, the same faint smell of candle smoke and old polish. And yet... something had shifted.

It was in the air—like that stillness just before the first drop of rain. Like something was holding its breath.

Even Thérèse was quiet.

I sat in my usual spot, my phone in my pocket. I hadn't written for days—like there was nothing left to say. Which, for me, was saying something.

It felt like a slow descension to the centre of the earth—and a slow inner quiet ascension.

A blind Chinese woman entered. No cane, no dog. Just slow, confident steps across the church tiles, one hand trailing the backs of pews, the other holding a small plastic bag.

She didn't pause at the candles. Didn't look around. Just walked straight to the front, stood beneath the mosaic of Mary, and whispered, "Thank you."

That was it.

Then she sat. Not in prayer, not in grief. Just... presence. Like she'd arrived and that was enough.

I watched her for a long while. She didn't move, didn't speak again. But something about her stillness unsettled me in the best way.

"You feel it too," said Thérèse.

I nodded. "What is it?"

"It's what happens when you stop expecting lightning and start noticing dew."

The candles glowed more than usual, as if aware they were being watched. One burned low—slow and steady, refusing to flicker.

The door creaked open. A young man entered with a nervous gait. Behind him, a mother carrying her baby. Then an older couple I'd seen before, but never together. One by one, they came.

Quiet, unsure, each one carrying something invisible.

I'd spent weeks watching people pray, wish, cry, light, leave. But today, I didn't want to watch. I wanted to stay.

I whispered, "I'm listening with all my senses."

Thérèse didn't reply.

She didn't have to.

It didn't take long for my senses to drag me into my novelist world.

The blind lady reminded me of Lucy Wang—an 'adults only' hairdresser-artist from Amsterdam. I smiled, recalling the stillness of my mind when I wrote about her. That day, I gained literary clarity after a sexual climax—a solo one. The words flew from places I didn't know existed, but gave me creative power far beyond my own imagination.

As a novelist, I am not a runaway boy, nor a runaway man.

I am present.

Under control, but not controlled.

Wild, authentic, and raw.

That's where I found my voices.

The one for love.

The controversial one.

The one I'm being criticised for now.

The one no one can take away from me.

Chapter 30

No Holy Value At All

It wasn't a pulled muscle.

Wasn't a blister.

Wasn't the result of hiking through Belgian dunes or scaling church towers.

It was just... sore.

A deep, slow ache in both thighs—like I'd walked too far from myself, and now my body was calling me back.

At first, I blamed the shoes. Then the footpath. Then the cheap mattress in the flat. But none of those excuses felt honest.

So I stopped.

Mid-walk. Middle of the day. In the middle of a street I didn't know the name of.

I found a bench near a florist—half in sun, half in shadow—and sat. Properly sat. Not just to check my phone. Not to tie a shoe. Just... to sit.

It felt awkward.

People hurried past like ants with agendas. Bags bouncing against their hips. Mouths full of half-eaten sandwiches and business calls. No one sat.

And I realised—I hadn't really rested in days.

Not properly.

Even when I was still, I was clenching somewhere: jaw, shoulders, chest. Even my ankles had opinions.

My legs weren't sore from walking too much.

They were sore from never stopping long enough to heal.

The body has a funny way of whispering. Then complaining. Then shouting. And when you don't listen, it sends the message somewhere else—into dreams, skin, the silence between heartbeats.

I closed my eyes and tried something I hadn't done in a long time.

I asked my body how it was doing.

It didn't answer in words.

But something inside me ached silently.

Later that day, I bought soup. Real soup. Not from a tin, not microwaved, not rushed.

It came with bread that had to be torn apart slowly. I ate it alone at a table by a window—no phone, no noise, no pretending I was anywhere else.

The soup didn't fix everything.

But it reminded me I was worth feeding.

That evening, back in the church, I just sat on the wooden pew and let my bones belong to the moment.

I unlaced my shoes slowly.

Then I placed both feet on the ground—evenly, fully.

And rested.

A steamed halo marked this event on the polished floor.

It felt good—very good indeed—until my self-awareness decided to question the core of my restlessness.

It became ugly instantly.

My siblings and I were raised on the idea that we only exist if we do things.

We had to be busy for the sake of it, and gain status from it.

There was no "to be"—only "to do."

It never made any sense—especially when your doings didn't contribute to personal or collective growth.

We were doing things out of habit.

We were stupidity on legs.

"I did that" versus "I am that."

"I do" versus "I am"—at its simplest form.

No one took the time to question our being versus our doing.

No one took the time to question the "I am" as a self-evolutionary entity—as the core of all human evolution.

A small five-second rest could have changed the rest of our familial existence—and destiny.

Most of my life, I sought refuge in my doings to avoid the ugliness of not being whole.

Now I've flipped the coin.

I am, and I have trouble settling into my doings—except for writing.

Seeking existence has had its fair share of challenges, pain, and invisible rewards.

My eyes rested on the structural lightness of the Gothic arches—which somehow symbolised someone's five-second pause in the history of architecture.

From monolithic to skeletal structures, to achieve greater

spans, bigger spaces, better light, and endless, pure, holy sensory experiences.

This engineering prowess didn't happen overnight—it took over a century to perfect, through countless adjustments, disasters, and unaccounted human losses.

But it all started with a pause.

A pause that challenged the status quo and the beliefs of past generations.

There is no act of creation if our being isn't included in our doing.

These words are not the words of God, but mine.

After reading Thérèse's letters, I'm well aware that the size of our doings is irrelevant.

But the size of our being isn't negotiable.

All in, around the clock.

Whatever the weather.

Whatever the challenge.

Whatever it takes to transcend to oneness.

Without the authenticity of the "be", the "do" has no value.

No holy value at all.

TWO EURO CANDLES

Chapter 31

Not Bloody Moonwalking

He rolled in like he owned the aisle.

He is a local. Mid-seventies, maybe older. Beard like a retired magician and a dirty scarf tucked neatly around his neck. His wheelchair had duct tape on one armrest and a bumper sticker on the back that read: "Not dead yet."

He parked right in front of the candle rack. Sat there for a while. Didn't light anything. Just looked.

Then he said, "Alright, Mary. If you're listening—and I know you are—I'd like my legs back. Or at least a better chair. Preferably one with brakes."

Thérèse perked up. "Oh, this is going to be good."

He fished out a coin and shoved it into the box like he was

tipping a bartender. Then, with shaky hands, lit a candle. It flared high, burned bright. He didn't flinch.

Then—no joke—the chair moved.

Just a nudge. Backwards.

He froze. Looked behind him. Then forward again.

The chair rolled back another two feet.

He slammed his palms on the wheels and said, "Oi. This better not be your idea of a miracle."

The chair kept moving. Slow. Smooth. Dead straight. Backwards.

Everyone in the church turned to look.

And then, just like that and maybe out of fear, he stood up.

Not confidently. Not triumphantly. More like someone testing ice. But he stood.

The entire church gasped. A woman whispered "Mon Dieu!" like we'd all slipped into a French documentary.

He took three steps forward.

The chair rolled back two more behind him like it was retreating respectfully.

He looked at Mary. "I said legs, not bloody moonwalking."

Thérèse laughed so hard I swear one of the candles wobbled. "Well," she said, "he didn't specify direction."

He sat back down, slowly, carefully. Wiped his eyes. I couldn't tell if he was laughing or crying. Maybe both.

Before leaving, he turned to Mary and said out loud, "I'll be back tomorrow. Could you organise a helmet for me?"

And out he rolled. Backwards.

The church didn't go wild. No clapping, no gospel choir appearing out of nowhere. Just silence. Thick and strange.

Then one of the priests stepped out from the shadows and said, "Well. That's new."

I lit a candle on credit without thinking. For what, I wasn't sure. Maybe out of habits. Maybe for all of us who ask for a miracle and get something slightly off—but still wonderful.

Thérèse whispered, "Miracles don't always make sense. They just make movement."

I acknowledged Thérèse's wisdom, but I was in a hurry that day.

I made my way to the train station and boarded a train to Bruges.

I wasn't the only one. The sun invited everyone to warm their heart in the Venice of the North. The carriage was full. Only one seat left in front of a backpacker well asleep, and curled up in the corner seat, hood pulled halfway over his head, backpack wedged between his knees like a life raft. Early twenties, maybe. Smelled faintly of hostel detergent and a bad morning breath blended into energy drink artificial flavours.

And my God, the noise.

It wasn't even a proper snore. It was a warbling, nasal purr that sounded like a tired chainsaw trying to remember its purpose.

Having no choice, I sat opposite him, headphones ready. No luck. Volume up. Still no good. I could feel the sound in my molars.

We pulled out of Ostend station and I debated changing seats. But the carriage was full. Students. Tourists. A nun scrolling on an iPad. All of them somehow managing to ignore the noise that had hijacked my skull.

The trip to Bruges was barely 20 minutes odyssey with delays. So, I resigned. I turned to stare out the window. Fields. Factories. Brief flashes of cows in profile. All blurred by the rhythm of one stranger's desperate attempt to suck in sleep.

I sighed loudly, hoping the sound would pierce the dream-fog and wake him gently.

He snored louder.

And then—I laughed.

Out of nowhere.

A real laugh. Not angry. Not bitter. Just honest.

Because here was this kid, completely surrendered to rest. Unbothered. Unapologetic. He was asleep like the world hadn't yet convinced him to be polite about it.

And me? I was a grown man on holiday getting upset because someone else had found rest in public.

I let go.

Closed my eyes. Let the sound wash over me.

It didn't stop. But I stopped fighting it.

Somewhere near the outskirt of Jabbeke, he stirred. Snorted himself half-awake. Blinked at me blearily.

"Sorry, man," he said, rubbing his eyes. "Do I snore?"

"Yes," I said. "A lot."

He grinned innocently.

Then went back to sleep.

No fuss. Just freedom.

I wrote in my phone:

> *I make noise too.*
>
> *And maybe grace doesn't ask us to be quiet.*
>
> *Maybe it just asks us to keep breathing.*
>
> *Even loudly.*

Chapter 32

Sort Me Out, Mary

She came in like a storm front.

Red-faced. Fast steps. A handbag that swung like a weapon. She stomped past the pews, nearly knocked over a rack of brochures, and muttered a stream of profanities so creative it deserved subtitles.

Her husband followed five steps behind, carrying a coat she clearly didn't want.

She marched straight up to the candle rack, shoved a coin into the box like it had personally offended her, and lit the flame with all the delicacy of a barbecue lighter at a bogan birthday.

Then she said—loudly—"Sort me out, Mary. Or I swear I'm gonna punch someone."

Thérèse hummed in my head. "A true daughter of fire."

The woman stood there, breathing like she'd just run from a parking fine. Her husband hovered awkwardly by the side altar, pretending to examine a pamphlet on sacred music.

She closed her eyes. One second. Two. Ten.

And then—just like that—she softened.

Her shoulders dropped. Her jaw unclenched. She blinked like someone waking from a long, unpleasant dream.

She turned around, walked back to her husband, took the coat from his arms, and said—softly—"Let's go get lunch."

He looked like he'd seen a ghost. Or a miracle. Maybe both.

They left hand in hand. Slowly. Quietly.

I stared at the candle. It hadn't flickered once.

"She was terrifying," I said to Thérèse.

"She was grieving," she replied. "Most fury is. People just forget how to translate it."

I sat there, thinking about how many people walk around carrying heat they don't know how to cool. How anger can be armour. How sometimes it melts—not with logic, but with light.

The church had already returned to its usual rhythm. Quiet movement. Small prayers. Candles burning down, one drip at a time.

I lit one of my own, thinking of all the rage I'd swallowed in my life. Some of it justified. Some of it just noise.

Thérèse said, "It's not about losing your anger. It's about giving it somewhere safe to land."

That was the sentence I needed to hear.

I went back to the Airbnb and addressed the elephant in the room—the one that had consumed me since January 17th, 2025.

I sat on my bed and wrote to myself:

> *At the time, my inner observer invited me not to dance. Not to react. Just to pause, to see if the fire would also consume itself into nothing.*

> *It was very hard not to dance after reading the headline in a national newspaper—and the 422 online comments on an article that judged me without inviting me into the conversation.*

> *I promised myself I wouldn't become a keyboard warrior. My daughter begged me not to poke the bear. So, I took my book out of sale—just to see what would happen next.*

> *Nothing happened.*

> *Except it gave me time to edit the book a couple more times. And to reflect on the fact that most of those online comments were made by people who hadn't read my novel.*

> *Fewer than twenty units had been sold organically prior to the newspaper publication.*

I never expected that 'Ostend' would be approved by the Australian Classification Board for its literary, creative and cultural merit.

I sought the Board's guidance, process and procedure to ensure I was on the right side of the law.

Secondly, I wanted my book to be labelled correctly—so I wouldn't offend anyone.

The sticker "Mature–Unrestricted" was meant to act as a gatekeeper.

Writing about domestic violence and rape wasn't easy. But somehow—it was.

Because I experienced all of it.

'Ostend' is a coded version of my personal story.

At fourteen, I never imagined that being raped would one day give me literary, creative, and cultural merit.

Being raped in the back of a blue Toyota Corolla station wagon on a small country road was an awful experience.

The person who raped me was a gambler—like the ones who raped Nikolina Koval in 'Ostend'.

He gambled his cosy family life for a fifteen-minute paedophile thrill.

He knew where to go.

He knew how to do it.

And he knew that my father—a policeman, the harshest man in town—wore the nickname "The Sheriff" with pride.

The reality is, my rapist didn't gamble at all—I was a safe bet.

He was well aware that I was afraid of my father and an easy target who would never report his actions or crimes.

He was right.

I never found the courage or the guts to face my father—or seek his help.

Being raped was better than being dead.

No joke.

Whatever the circumstances, it would have been my fault.

Silence is survival.

Every week, for years, my rapist consumed me visually.

He was the maintenance officer at the local public pool.

During a routine inspection in the boys' change room, he once told me "He liked my small penis."

The weekly compulsory swimming lessons were more than uncomfortable.

Most of the kids received the same visual treatment.

In our tiny Lycra, we were fresh meat—ready for consumption.

After migrating to Australia in 1996, I had a mental

breakdown—the kind that contemplates the edge of a cliff.

I sought help.

My story came out, revealed behind closed doors in a moment of intimacy.

As a teenager who loved motorcycles, Metzeler tyres, and modified exhaust pipes, the only words I used or thought of to explain how I felt about my rape were: "He was moving hectically like a piston in a too-small cylinder chamber."

Sadly, it sounded technical.

Technically painful.

But they were my words.

Not snippets printed in a national newspaper.

My words.

Within context.

The ones that recounted.

My physical pain.

My shame.

My silence.

My guilt.

My endless fears.

Funnily enough, I never held much resentment toward my rapist.

But I can't say the same about my father.

Because he wasn't there for me.

He wasn't there for me—as a man.

He wasn't there for me—as a father.

He wasn't the law.

He wasn't love.

He was a waste.

He was the one who, consciously or not, stuck a sign on my forehead that read: "I am fearful and easy to rape."

And for that, I've wished again and again that someone had killed him out of my life—everyone's lives.

As an adult runaway boy, I sought answers.

I went to seminars, retreats, conventions, healers of all kinds.

There, I met people with similar pasts—or worse.

I met victims of domestic violence by the dozen.

Raped men and women by the hundreds.

They exist—I met them.

Most of them wish they didn't exist.

Most of them wish they were see-through.

Most are voiceless, quietly seeking resolution.

How many didn't make it to the seminars, the retreats, the conventions?

Those ones are symbolised in 'The Ostend Diaries'.

Life without names.

Purchased innocence.

Horror well beyond our imagination.

They exist—I didn't meet them.

We know about them—Usually, when it's too late.

When their names appear on newspaper headlines.

I've been lucky.

I can talk about it.

I can write about it.

And I'm okay with it if you don't like my rawness or my authenticity.

The Gaston, the Ludo, and the Florian drive blue Toyota Corolla station wagons.

They're not just characters in a fictitious novel.

They drive our streets.

They exist—I met one of them.

He was a family man.

Like many in the French Pelicot's story.

TWO EURO CANDLES

Chapter 33

Stop Asking for Lottery Numbers

He came in again—third time this week—same jacket, same ritual.

Baseball cap pulled low, wearing sunglasses indoors like he was hiding from God and the tax office. He walked up to the candle stand like it owed him money.

Dropped in two euros with flair, lit a candle, muttered: "This time, Mary. Just give me six numbers. That's all I'm asking."

Thérèse groaned in my head. "Oh, not him again."

Apparently, he'd been doing this for months. Every Tuesday and Saturday. Always just before the draw. Always the same prayer.

"Make me rich, make it quick, amen."

He even tried different tactics—lighting three candles in a row, rearranging the stand, whispering the names of former winners.

Once, he placed a scratchie next to the statue. As an offering.

"I don't even mind sharing the winnings," he'd said. "I'll give 5% to the poor. Or 3% if the jackpot's massive."

Thérèse sounded exhausted. "He thinks I'm the patron saint of Lotto syndicates."

To be fair, he wasn't the only one. I'd heard others ask for "financial clarity", which was code for please cancel my credit card debt.

One man had even prayed for "a career that pays well and doesn't involve talking to people."

I couldn't tell if people were praying or pitching.

Still, something about Mr Lotto stuck with me.

He wasn't greedy—not really. Just desperate.

He wanted freedom. Escape. A second chance, paid upfront.

"He doesn't trust slow miracles," said Thérèse. "He wants fireworks. Most people do."

"What's wrong with that?"

"Nothing. Unless they miss the sparkler already burning in their hand."

The next morning, I passed the man outside the church. I couldn't help it—I asked if he'd had any luck.

With some humility, he pulled out a collection of lottery tickets from his wallet. He hadn't won. Again.

He sighed, folded the papers neatly, put them back in his wallet, and said, "Maybe next week."

Then, before walking off, he added, "I thank Mary anyway."

And that—more than anything—broke me a little.

Because even after disappointment, he still said thanks.

Not to a priest. Not to a system. Just to something beyond him.

I whispered to the universe, "Help him notice the miracle that doesn't come with a jackpot."

I reckoned if Thérèse was around, she'd be smiling at my two cents' worth of street wisdom.

Any holy insight is always a good excuse for coffee and keyboard writing.

Caruso was again my café of choice.

I was nursing beautifully crafted pastries and a reflective mood, while leafing through a newspaper left behind by a man who'd ordered one black coffee and stared at the wall like it owed him something.

A horoscope.

Not something I usually read.

I used to—like a desperate addiction.

All signs were tucked between an ad for cholesterol pills and a cartoon that hadn't been funny since 2002.

So I scrolled past Gemini, skipped Scorpio. Landed on Libra—mine.

It read:

"You are waiting for someone to tell you it's okay to begin."

That was it.

No lucky numbers. No love forecast. No mention of financial windfalls or impending disappointment.

Just that sentence.

I reread it six times.

Because it knew me.

More than any star ever could.

Without much discretion, I tore up the paper like it was mine.

Cut off Virgo's legs.

Trimmed Scorpio's head.

Slimmed the cholesterol ad.

A new beginning was in my hand.

A small offering from God, neatly folded in my wallet.

A spiritual lottery ticket now tucked into my jacket pocket.

It was something sacred.

Unique. Present. Instantaneous.

I'd been waiting for permission my whole bloody life.

To quit.

To start.

To write.

To rest.

To say "I love you."

To love myself—freely.

I could trace every delay, every missed chance, every quiet ache in my chest back to that single impulse: waiting.

Waiting for a sign—for someone older or wiser or more spiritually hydrated to say, "Yes, go. You're allowed now."

And now here it was. In size 8 font. On newsprint.

My permission slip.

I spent the afternoon walking along the beach. Cold wind. Screaming gulls. Sand in my socks.

I kept pulling out the paper. Reading the line again... and again.

You are waiting for someone to tell you it's okay to begin.

Later, at the church, I didn't light a candle.

I took the horoscope clipping, folded it twice, and tucked it under the corner of the donation box. Like a message in a bottle.

For someone else.

Or maybe just for me, again.

In my phone, I wrote:

> *If I'm looking for signs,*
>
> *I'm not listening.*
>
> *If I'm waiting for permission,*
>
> *I'm not living.*
>
> *Begin anyway.*
>
> *Begin every day.*

Then I went back to my accommodation, made a cup of tea, and started writing another chapter I'd been avoiding for years.

Not because I knew what to say.

But because it was time.

Chapter 34

Goodbye, Brave Soldier

It wasn't raining when I got there.

Bit of a breeze, sure. Grey clouds loafing about like they couldn't decide whether to bother. But inside the church, it was dry. Quiet. The usual: faint incense, footsteps on stone, candles flickering politely.

Then the umbrella opened.

Loud. Sharp. Sudden.

Everyone jumped—including the woman who owned it. Mid-sixties, smart coat, nice boots, eyes wide like she'd just been goosed by the Holy Spirit.

She hadn't touched it. I swear.

One moment it was resting on the floor, closed as anything.

Next minute—snap—up it popped, right there beside the pews.

People stared. A kid gasped.

And then—just to make things even stranger—a fine mist started falling. Indoors. Inside the church. From absolutely nowhere.

It was a light illusion. But it felt wholly real. Surreal, indeed.

Thérèse muttered, "Oh, for heaven's sake. Subtlety, please!"

I looked up. Only outside: cold, soft rain drumming the windows. Inside: God's blurry presence, for less than a minute. But enough to make a point.

The woman stood under her umbrella, blinking up at the mosaic of Mary like she'd been caught in the middle of something personal.

She didn't run. Didn't scream. She laughed. A sharp, nervous bark that turned into proper chuckling. She turned slowly in a circle, then whispered, "Alright. Message received."

Then it stopped. Just like that.

No thunder. No rainbow. Just stillness.

The woman folded her umbrella, sat back down, and crossed herself with a kind of giddy reverence.

She didn't light a candle. She didn't need to.

After a moment, someone else—bold as brass—walked up to

the candle stand and said, "I'll have whatever she's having."

Thérèse was in stitches. "That's what happens when God gets playful. Makes a scene, clears the air, leaves no explanation."

I looked around. Everyone had gone a bit quiet. Not scared. Just... curious.

Like they'd all remembered, for a moment, that magic might still be on the table.

"Miracles don't always fall from the sky," I said softly.

"Sometimes they do," said Thérèse. "Just enough to get your hair wet."

Outside, it was the kind of wind that didn't tap politely on your coat collar—it punched.

I'd only made it twenty metres towards the bakery before it hit, turning the world into a slapstick comedy.

Leaves skidded across the cobblestones like frantic crabs. A café awning flapped with such fury I thought it might take flight. And my umbrella—poor, faithful, €9.95 fold-up from the newsagent—took its final stand.

It went quickly.

One gust, then a full inversion—ribs snapped, canopy flipped. It looked like a startled spider having an existential crisis.

I held it up like a wounded flag, unsure whether to fight for it or toss it into the next bin and salute its service while whispering, "Goodbye, brave soldier."

Two women laughed at me from across the street. Not cruelly. Just honestly.

Without moving, I joined them. I laughed too.

Loud.

There was nothing else to do.

For the first time in weeks, I laughed so hard I had to stop walking. Bent over, hands on my knees, drenched, ridiculous—and lighter than I'd felt in ages.

Something broke open in me then.

Not just like the Chinese-made umbrella—something deeper.

That part of me that had been holding on too tightly to the idea that life owed me neatness.

Predictability.

Dry socks.

Back at the flat, I hung my coat over the heater and made tea.

And then—because something about destruction always leaves a bit of space behind—I cleaned the little kitchenette. Properly. No distractions. No phone.

Just the sound of the kettle and the rain tap-dancing on the window.

The wild outside world called me back.

I left my phone and wallet inside.

I just needed to feel freedom. Pure, laughing joy.

It didn't take long for my hair to drip. My shoes to squelch.

People gave me a look that hovered somewhere between pity and amusement.

I smiled.

I laughed loudly, like kids do when they're allowed to.

And I thought—maybe this is it.

Not transcendence. Not clarity.

Just the quiet revelation that nothing needs to go perfectly for something holy to happen.

I felt invigorated.

Energised.

More than alive.

I walked home in the rain.

And didn't rush.

Made a long detour.

A street puddle became a trampoline made of joy.

I bounced into life.

Laughed out loud.

Invited strangers to do the same.

Some laughed.

Some smiled.

Some shook their heads in disbelief.

They didn't see my joy.

Only their life limitations.

Chapter 35

It's Taken Care Of

They came in like clockwork that day—three separate people, three very different prayers, one shared tone: "Fix it, now."

The first was a teenager in a school uniform, lighting a candle while still wearing his earbuds. He muttered, "Please let me pass maths tomorrow... I swear I'll study after."

He lit the candle and walked out before the flame had settled.

"Didn't even take the headphones out," I said.

"Miracles are not cheat sheets," Thérèse huffed. "You don't get divine downloads while skipping the homework."

Next came a woman, maybe late thirties, clearly frustrated. She looked around to make sure no one was listening and whispered, "Can you just send me the right man? I'm exhausted."

She lit her candle with the energy of someone returning something she'd bought online.

And finally—a businessman. Slick and nervous. Candle lit. Eyes tight. "Please let her forget what I said last night."

"Ah," Thérèse sighed. "Classic damage-control theology."

I leaned back in the chair and whispered, "Why does everyone treat prayer like an Uber Eats order?"

"Because they're scared," she said. "And because they've forgotten that most real miracles come wrapped in effort."

"What's the miracle, then?"

"Showing up. Staying. Doing the work."

I looked around the church. So many candles lit for things people wanted to skip—grief, exams, awkward conversations, real love, hard choices.

They weren't bad people. Just tired. And human.

The woman came back ten minutes later and blew out her own candle. "Too late," she muttered.

I couldn't tell if she meant the prayer or the romance.

"You ever skip the hard parts?" I asked.

"Of course," said Thérèse. "Once I prayed for humility and accidentally got the flu. God is hilarious."

I smiled. Then walked to the candle rack and lit one for myself.

Not to skip anything.

But to stay.

To try.

And maybe even to fail—the long way around.

My Ostend routine is well settled now. Coffees. Writing. Editing. Walking. Observing my thoughts and feelings.

Being surprised by their softness.

Writing. Editing. Eating.

It wasn't a lavish meal. Just soup and bread with salted butter. Another coffee. No dessert.

The kind of lunch you have when you're trying to be gentle with yourself but not too indulgent—like you're still negotiating whether you deserve comfort.

I'd eaten quietly in the corner of a café just off Wapenplein. No phone. No distractions. Just watching people walk past the windows, wondering if I looked as aimless as they did.

When I asked for the bill, the waiter smiled.

"It's taken care of."

I blinked.

"Sorry?"

He leaned in, whispered like it was a conspiracy. "Someone paid for you."

I looked around. No one I recognised. No knowing glances. No kind stranger lingering for a thank you.

"Do you know who?"

He shrugged. "They said just to say—'You looked like you needed it.'"

I stood there, stunned.

Not out of joy. Not even gratitude.

At first, I was... suspicious.

I checked my pockets. Phone? Wallet? All there.

Then I checked myself.

Why was my first response doubt?

Why couldn't I just accept it—this small, anonymous act of grace?

I left the café with a full stomach and an unsettled heart.

Walked for over an hour, letting the wind slap the questions out of me.

Why did I find it so hard to receive?

I'd spent years trying to earn everything.

Love. Rest. Kindness.

As though anything unearned were debts.

But this—this was a gift.

Not earned. Not explained. Not transactional.

Just given.

All my life, I have been a giver.

Freely giving, without much thought.

That's how I am.

A giver. A carer.

And now... a receiver.

"You looked like you needed it."

What did they mean?

What does it mean to receive—freely, anonymously?

I usually feel ashamed.

Deeply ashamed.

At an early age, I learned quickly that I could only count on myself in life.

Help or offering made me uncomfortable.

Very out of place.

It wasn't me.

Receiving felt like someone had decided on my behalf.

Without consultation.

Forced on to me.

Like it was when I was a kid.

No one was interested in my voice or opinions.

There were no offerings—just orders to comply with.

Was this another of Thérèse's invitations to surrender?

Counting only on myself—it's like walking on fine ice.

Never knowing when it will crack.

When you will drown.

When you will survive survival.

Today's offering felt like a bridge to God's generosity.

A path to a better life—or at least better conditions.

Someone has my back.

I am not alone anymore.

I close my eyes. I feel confused.

Blessed. Ashamed. Light. Heavy. Alone. Lost. Poor. Rich. Sad. Happy. Shallow. Complete. Teary.

It's all too much for me.

My blood pressure joined the party—not a good sign.

To regain control, I walked, I lit a candle.

Not in thanks.

But in surrender.

I whispered, "I'm sorry it took me so long to say yes to kindness. I didn't understand what it meant to receive. I still don't. But I'll do my best to unlearn my learning."

The flame shivered once. Held strong.

Back at the Airbnb, I collapsed in the shower cubicle.

My tears were filling the North Sea.

High tides weren't expected—but they were coming fast now.

With my naked butt cheeks squashed against the tiled floor, I was again one of many younger versions of myself—looking to receive love that never came. Or at least not in a form I could enjoy.

I realised that throughout life, unconsciously or not, I had closed my hands.

Nothing could land in them.

Receiving wasn't me.

Only closed fists—to fight, to provide, to sustain, to survive.

Still slumped in the shower tub, I stretched my hands wide open—a signal to my reactive behaviours that everything I've learned to date is now on notice.

A disposal notice, indeed.

Later, I wrote:

Someone saw me.

Not my face.

Not my failings.

Just the part that needed something

and didn't know how to be.

And for once,

I let it be.

Chapter 36

Interview With The Invisible

He had a notebook. Of course he did.

Journalist. Local. Fringed scarf, sharp haircut, voice like he thought in headlines. He introduced himself with a handshake that was all confidence and curiosity.

"I'm writing a piece on unusual places of meaning," he said. "Bit of human interest, bit of culture. The whole 'why do people still believe?' question."

I pointed him to the pews. "Plenty of people to watch."

"And what about you?" he asked. "You part of the staff?"

I almost laughed. "No, just here often enough to be furniture."

He smirked. Sat beside me. Watched an old woman light three candles—one for each of her grandkids, apparently.

"So, who are they praying to?" he asked, scribbling something. "Is it about God? Ritual? Habit?"

"Sometimes it's grief," I said. "Sometimes hope. Sometimes just a place to sit and not fall apart."

Thérèse whispered, "Let him squirm a bit."

The journalist walked up to the statue, looked at it like it owed him a quote. Then back at the candle rack. He hovered a while.

"I don't get it," he said. "It's just a building. And flames."

I didn't bother correcting him.

Then, without warning, he reached into his coat and pulled out two euros. Lit a candle. Just stood there.

Didn't say a word.

Didn't take notes.

He sat down again beside me, eyes softer now. "No idea why I did that."

"You don't need one," I said.

He jotted something quickly, then closed the notebook. "Alright," he muttered. "That's enough for today."

As he left, I caught a glimpse of what he'd written at the top of the page:

The Church That Breathes

Thérèse smiled in the back of my mind. "Everyone's a believer for ten seconds. The trick is remembering how that felt."

I thought numerous times about what it meant to witness faith without understanding it. How awe doesn't need a manual.

Some things just need to be felt. Or lit. Or left unnamed.

The whole thing reminded me of a grandmother and her two granddaughters. I observed them a few months ago, during a previous trip to Ostend—well before Thérèse and I ventured into the greatness and vastness of the rabbit hole of my holy education.

The trio left an uneasy footprint in my imagination, but deep inside, I questioned their true reasons and motives for being in front of Mary in the first place.

My impression at the time was that the grandmother used Mary like a state-of-the-art human car wash.

Deep clean and protective treatments in no time.

I pulled out my phone, scrolled through my 2023/24 journal entries, and pleased my mind just reading about the mysterious three.

> *The woman entered in a flurry of motion and designer wool. Her heels clicked sharply on the stone floor, a pointed rhythm out of step with the hush of the sacred space. Her scent arrived before her—amber and tuberose, perfume so fine it cost more than most people's weekly wage. But there was something acidic beneath it: the scent of panic, of desperation masked by class.*

She dragged the two girls behind her, her gloved hands gripping theirs too tightly. The younger child, no older than seven, wore a pink beanie, her other hand clenched around the hem of her coat like it could protect her from what she didn't understand. The older girl, perhaps ten, had a stiff posture, her chin slightly raised, the echo of resistance already forming in her small body.

Their grandmother didn't speak to them as they walked—she pulled.

The woman was around sixty, though every inch of her attire suggested an aggressive defence against the passage of time. High-collared merino, boots tailored to her calves, and sunglasses too large for the muted light inside. Her hair was a perfectly stiff coif of silvery blonde, unmoved by the breeze or the emotion swelling beneath her skin.

Her face, however—despite its surgical interventions—was cracking.

Not with age, but with grief. With shame.

Her heels clicked once more, then skidded slightly against a tiny patch of water. She cursed under her breath, something clipped and French-sounding, then steadied herself and looked around. A few tourists were scattered through the pews. A couple near the front bowed in prayer. But no one looked up. That was good. That was necessary.

The light today was different. The stained-glass windows still cast colour, but muted. Outside, clouds dragged across the coast, dulling the brilliance into a spectral wash of deep blues and reds.

The church's smell was under attack—the woman's perfume overtook the damp stone and the oriental incense.

The rawness of hidden things stank.

She reached the left aisle and moved fast, half-walking, half-marching, her daughters' daughters in tow. The older one stumbled slightly, and the woman yanked her upright without breaking stride.

Her mind was a cacophony.

Her facial expression spoke millions of words—raw anger, betrayal, and disloyalty.

She rounded the final pew and reached the small alcove where Mary, serene and shimmering, waited in her wall of mosaic. The pale terracotta glazing caught the thin light like snow, outlining Mary's sorrowful gaze.

But the woman didn't see beauty.

She saw judgment.

She saw a mother. A harsh mother. A mother she knew.

The black steel candle stand stood like a miniature pyre beneath Mary's open arms. Several flames already danced in their fragile glasses. The woman lurched toward it and let go of the girls.

They stood awkwardly, side by side, stiff and watchful. The younger girl lowered her head. The older one did not. She rolled her eyes. She didn't want to be there.

The woman began to rattle through her handbag, the noise jarring in the silence—metallic, frantic, desperate.

Lipstick cases, receipts, gold credit cards, a tin of mints. Then coins.

She scraped up whatever she could find—one-euro pieces, a couple of fifties, two twos. She dropped them all into the donation slot in one frantic clatter, not counting, not caring.

It must be done. There is no way back. It's an emergency. A holy one.

She bought as many candles as she could, stacking the white shafts in her trembling hands. Her gloves were off now, stuffed into the handbag's mouth like the innards of an animal.

Her hands—once manicured and photographed—were shaking with rage and helplessness.

She lit candle after candle, fingers fumbling with the tiny sticks of fire, her lips moving, whispering things no one else could hear:

Please let them forget. Let them grow whole. Let no one ever know. Let this end. Let this end. Let this end.

Then she pushed the girls forward—physically moved them by their shoulders—until they stood before Mary. The little one looked up, confused, as her grandmother made the sign of the cross over her.

She did it again, faster. Then again, whispering in French:

Bénie sois-tu. Pardonne. Protège. Guéris.

The older girl stared forward, unblinking, jaw clenched.

Her grandmother placed a hand on her head, tried to press it down in a mock genuflection.

The girl resisted. Shoulders stiffened.

The woman's lips moved faster now, her voice a low hiss—not prayers, but a plea for silence. For secrecy. For erasure.

Raising her sunglasses onto her forehead, she looked to Mary now with eyes like a storm—pleading, enraged, splintered.

Do something. Say something. Fix this. Take it away.

She blinked.

Tears burned in her vision but didn't fall.

Not here. Not publicly.

The shame clung to her like the wool of her coat. Even now, she couldn't be seen to feel.

Not too much. Not like them.

It had to stay behind closed doors, filed away like an inconvenient bill.

The girls stood frozen.

The little one had begun to shake slightly—almost imperceptibly— her small hand reaching for her sister's.

The older girl took it.

The woman stepped back and quickly made the sign of the cross over herself.

Then, wordless, she reached for the girls again.

The older one flinched. The younger followed.

They turned.

She didn't look back at Mary.

She didn't look at the candles she'd lit.

She walked back the way she came—fast-paced, heels clacking once more, echoing down the aisle like punctuation marks on a letter she would never send.

Chapter 37

I'm Still Talking To Myself

It started as a hum.

Barely a murmur—just under breath—as I walked along the narrow stretch between the tram tracks and the seafront.

I was talking to myself again.

Not out loud, exactly. But not entirely silent either.

Half-muttered phrases. Rehearsed confessions. Imagined arguments I'd never have the courage to start.

It was three-quarters of the way between dancing and observing my life's content.

It was observing—with some form of manipulation.

"You're alright, mate."

"Bit much today, hey?"

"You really said that? God, you're an idiot."

It was automatic. Unfiltered.

Some sentences I didn't even recognise as mine.

There was a time I would've been embarrassed.

Would've shoved my hands in my pockets and looked away, as if pretending not to hear yourself makes the inner noise less real.

But that day, I let it happen.

Kept walking.

Kept speaking.

Responded, even.

It wasn't dramatic—no great reckoning, no epiphany. Just a slow realisation:

I was not losing my mind.

I was learning to stay inside it.

To tend to it.

To treat it like a place worth listening to.

I'd always imagined self-talk was meant to be positive.

That healing sounded like mantras and affirmations and the kind of language they put on fridge magnets.

But mine didn't sound like that.

Mine sounded like old self-therapy.

It sounded human.

Not fragile.

Not robust.

Just honest.

I passed a group of teenagers near the tram line. One of them said something in Flemish and laughed.

I smiled.

Not because I understood.

But because I didn't need to.

I'd spent so long trying to understand everyone else that I'd forgotten how to simply accompany myself.

That night, I walked into the church and didn't pray.

I never prayed—I allowed myself just to be holy, without the glory.

Just sat.

Let my mind chatter.

Let my inner voice ramble and unravel and say things it hadn't had a safe place to say in years.

Thérèse didn't intervene.

I think she kept quiet on purpose.

Let me have the room.

When I left, I felt no clarity.

Just a bit less tension in the jaw.

A little more flexibility in my body.

Some lightness in my heart.

And that was enough.

Later, I wrote:

> *Maybe healing isn't about shutting up the noise.*
>
> *Maybe it's about letting yourself talk long enough to hear what's underneath.*

Chapter 38

Joy And Hilarity

They came in holding hands. Mid-thirties. Kind faces. Worn at the edges.

She carried a small envelope. He carried silence.

They walked straight to the statue without fuss. Lit a single candle, heads bowed, barely breathing.

She whispered something. He didn't speak. Just nodded once, like he was afraid that if he opened his mouth, he'd fall apart.

I didn't need to hear the words. I'd seen the look before.

They wanted a child.

Thérèse was quiet. Reverent. "This one's heavy."

And then—out of nowhere—a runaway page boy, chased by

his mum, made his way towards the two-euro candle holder.

He was determined, and good entertainment.

His clenched hands were full of rose petals.

Feeling the pressure of his mum catching up with him, and not wanting to lose centre stage, he threw the petals at Mary.

Not many. Just a handful.

White. Soft. Floating down from Mary's feet like someone had dropped a blessing from the heavens.

Joy and hilarity joined the party.

Everyone stopped.

I laughed.

A tourist dropped her phone. A child pointed. An old man gasped.

The show stopped.

His mum apologised, trying to contain her boy and clean his floral mess at the same time.

The couple bent down to help her.

The women shared eye contact.

Invisible woman-language was spoken—understood.

The mum invited her boy to give the petals to the couple.

They needed them more than Mary.

He did so with pride—like he was also waiting for a friend to play with him.

God's special envoy disappeared.

The couple stood there—petals in hand.

They looked up—not surprised. Just calm.

Prayers had been answered.

I was tense, sitting on the edge of my chair.

Then the woman turned to her partner. Smiled.

A real, wide, no-makeup smile.

He reached for her hand again. Said nothing.

Then they walked out.

Lighter. Changed.

The candle they lit burned brighter than the others.

Steady. Defiant.

Their emotions had made them drop some of their offering.

A few petals landed around the pews.

I picked one up gently, half expecting it to vanish like something in a dream.

But it didn't.

It smelled like something between perfume, prayer, and reality.

I tucked it into my wallet. Just sat there in the hush, restraining myself from writing anything.

The church didn't move. No thunder. No voice.

But something had shifted again.

Something had been heard.

Thérèse whispered, "Sometimes grace falls before the answer."

"It always does," I answered.

When leaving the church, Thérèse's words echoed, amplified and resonated through my chest.

Humility was with me.

Not just humble—humbleness level 50,000—like the kind you reach when playing video games.

I felt small. But present.

Years ago, I found literary grace through the imagined life of Coco Carajuca, who embodied God's grace like no other—and sadly, she fell well before the answers—her answers.

Coco's spirit was my saviour—the one who kept the light burning through life's darkness. Without her, I probably wouldn't have survived the mental strain of an anti-corruption enquiry—which triggered the rawness—level 100,000—of my bottled emotions to erupt into such extreme creative form.

Grace fell before the answers when I learned that I wasn't a person of interest.

Relief had never been so deeply appreciated.

Unhealthy blood pressure and loss of vision were finally kept at bay.

Here in Ostend, I didn't know the page boy was part of a local gang. There were rose petals scattered along the footpath from the church doors as far as my eyes could see—tiny blush-coloured petals, soft as breath and absurdly out of place.

The wind hadn't carried them.

They'd been placed.

Or dropped.

Or offered.

I stopped walking.

Looked around.

My joy level hit 1,000,000.

Just a quiet Wednesday, and a scattering of something that felt too gentle for the grey.

I bent down. Picked one up.

It was real. Velvet to the touch. Fragrant.

Ridiculous in its beauty.

Unexplained.

And suddenly I thought of her.

Thérèse.

I thought of her like she was a secret girlfriend—I must admit, my thoughts rarely left her or her sayings.

She had been more than a tour guide on my holy introspection.

She had been the voice of simplicity and lightness.

She had been like a laundromat operator, inviting me to wash my fabricated identity away—as often as it took to discover the true colour of creation.

Her invitations to change were always generous, humorous, and gifted.

This insight made me feel like a winter leek in a frozen garden.

I stood there—stiff, motionless.

A man passed me. Gave me a look.

I grinned.

I stayed.

There's something unnerving about unasked-for beauty.

It demands nothing.

Answers to no mood.

Appears without agenda.

And in doing so, it disarms you.

That night, at the AirBnB, I lit a candle—not for a request.

Just a thank you.

Thank you for reminders.

Thank you for unearned gentleness.

Thank you for beauty that doesn't ask to be proven.

Later, I wrote:

> *Maybe I am a wild page boy bringing back the light to the motherland.*
>
> *Maybe I am the Holy Spirit paving new paths for generations to come.*
>
> *Maybe I am the beauty that doesn't need to be proven.*
>
> *Maybe I am unaware of the miracles I dispense.*

TWO EURO CANDLES

Chapter 39

The Voice Goes Quiet

She didn't show up that morning.

No quip. No whisper. No warm flicker at the edge of my thoughts. Just silence.

I waited—like someone left hanging on the end of a phone line that never connects.

Lit a candle. Walked the aisles. Sat in my usual spot.

Nothing.

The church was normal. Or maybe too normal. As if everything had returned to baseline, and I'd imagined the rest.

I typed into my phone out of habit:

Still here. Are you?

Nothing.

Maybe Thérèse didn't like my thoughts of her being my secret girlfriend.

Maybe she doesn't know that she is peace, wisdom, joy, serenity, and a calming abundance.

A woman near the altar began to cry. Not loudly. Just softly—the way grief leaks when it's tired.

I thought, Normally, Thérèse would've said something cheeky like, "That's the real incense."

But—silence.

I stared at Mary. Still. Stone. Remote.

Even the pigeons and seagulls outside were quiet.

I tried to joke. "What, gone on retreat? Lost interest? You running late, Saint?"

But the air held nothing but the faint scent of burnt wick and old wood.

I walked out. Down the street. Halfway to the bakery.

Then turned around.

Walked straight back in.

Still nothing.

That night, I dreamt of a dark garden. No flowers. Just soil. Damp. Still. Waiting.

The next morning—still no voice. No Thérèse.

Just me, the mosaic, and a single candle someone had forgotten to light.

So I lit it for them. Validated their wishes.

It burned slowly, as if pacing itself.

I sat beside it. Closed my eyes.

Didn't ask anything. Didn't push.

Just sat.

My melancholy and romanticism tried to infiltrate my mental space before my observer skills quietened them down.

And in that quiet—beyond thought, beneath noise—I felt something I couldn't name.

Not her voice. But her absence, filled with invitation.

Her nothingness blessed my heaviness.

Thankful, I was.

TWO EURO CANDLES

Chapter 40

But In Suggestion

When I slowed down into life, its magic appeared in forms and shapes I'd never imagined.

The instruments of everyday fiction convert normality into sensual, sensorial experiences.

Was it a dream or a hallucination?

It happened in the mirror.

I'd just stepped out of the shower, skin pink from the heat, the small bathroom thick with steam. The mirror was fogged over completely—just an abstract of breath and blur.

I wiped it with an old, dirty T-shirt of mine. A half-hearted swipe.

And saw it.

For the briefest moment, a shape behind me.

Faint. Human. Still.

I spun.

Nothing.

Of course.

But my heart didn't get the memo. It pounded like someone had knocked on it from the inside.

I stood there, wet, stupidly afraid, the towel slipping off my shoulder.

A part of me wanted to call out. Another part wanted to run.

But I did neither.

I just breathed.

Slowly realised—it was steam.

Probably.

It had moved with me. Reacted to the swipe. Maybe the heat had played a trick on my peripheral vision. Maybe I was just projecting—ghosts of grief, echoes of memory.

But still.

No bullshit.

There had been something.

I swore. I still do.

Later, dressed and calmer, I stared at the mirror again.

Nothing there but the shape of me and a few droplets edging to the bottom of the glass.

And I thought: Maybe this is how the divine works.

Not in thunder. Not in answers.

But in suggestion.

In the question we don't quite know how to ask.

Maybe it was the part of me I've tried not to see.

The part that still watches from the corner, waiting to be acknowledged.

To be named.

To be let in.

My friend Bruna, as a child, experienced an apparition of Mary.

A story she was never tired of sharing—with glowing eyes.

As a teenager, I was sceptical.

Mary, inside a tunnel, under a train track in remote Italy.

I was tempted to write another cinematic account of it, imagining "Presence of the Lord" by Eric Clapton as the soundtrack—intimately blessed by Yvonne Elliman's vocals.

But no. I gave my headspace a break—a leisurely bike ride

back to my body.

My face was red-burnt by the coldness of the North Sea wind.

I didn't care.

I laughed.

I cheered.

I surrendered.

I consented to the experience—to the present.

To God's miracles.

I rode my willingness and participation far beyond my teenage scepticism.

Everything was there.

Peace was between the North Sea and the sand dunes.

That day, I appeared.

To myself.

Chapter 41

Alone With The Statues

The doors creaked shut behind me. No tourists. No candles lit. No choir humming in rehearsal down the back. Just me and a lot of marble.

Even the fluorescent lights beside Mary were off. Only the old stained-glass windows let in a grey, cold sort of glow that made everything feel paused.

I sat in the fourth pew from the front. It's the one that doesn't wobble.

Phone in hand. Nothing to write.

No Thérèse. No warmth at the edge of my mind. No laughter.

Just statues. Still. Watching.

I looked at them properly for the first time—the saints in

stone and plaster, each caught mid-suffering or mid-serenity, all with eyes upturned like they were expecting a better ending.

They weren't beautiful. Not really. A bit dusty. Some cracks in the base. One had a chipped nose. I liked that.

At some point, I stretched out across the pew, resting my head where other people's coats usually go. It wasn't comfortable. But it felt... fair. Like maybe I didn't need to be useful today.

I closed my eyes. Listened.

Wind outside. Distant traffic. A creak in the rafters that sounded vaguely like a sigh.

No angels. No whispers. No divine slap on the back of the head.

But I stayed there anyway. Let the ache of being unanswered wash over me.

Thérèse's silence wasn't absence—it was invitation.

Something I needed to accept, and somehow appreciate.

Well, here I was.

Invited to what, I didn't know.

I felt defeated.

I moved to my usual chair—front row, second from the right, just under Thérèse's feet.

Something inside me said she would levitate today.

Thérèse and I, in no time, locked eyes firmly—before the gentleness of our thoughts did their magic.

My face relaxed.

Her eyes softened—smiled, even.

The combination of the red and blue light made her float gently at first, and I went full psychedelic in no time.

Thérèse had pleasure.

Intense floating pleasure.

I swore.

I was with her—floating madly.

Outside my body.

I was light.

Light—like a feather.

Light—like the flickering candles.

I don't remember how long it lasted—but it wasn't long enough.

The speed of light, I suppose.

When I landed back in reality, the light had shifted.

My internal light had shifted too.

I was still light-headed.

Weightless—maybe.

Someone had come in and lit a candle near Mary. I hadn't noticed.

I sat up slowly. Stiff. Cold.

Boiling—spiritually.

But not alone.

Chapter 42

The Receipt

I found it at the bottom of my coat pocket, folded into quarters and soft at the edges like it had been there longer than it should've.

A receipt.

2 waffles.

€6.10.

Timestamp: 13:04. An after-lunch sweetness.

Date: three weeks ago.

I didn't remember saving it. Didn't remember the waffles being particularly good either. Were they true Belgian waffles after all? But there it was—this small, wrinkled slip of proof that I'd been alive at a specific moment.

And for some reason, I couldn't throw it out.

I sat on the edge of the bed, unfolded it properly, smoothed it flat across my thigh. The ink was already starting to fade. Thermal paper always forgets faster than the heart.

I tried to recall the moment.

Where had I sat? Was it raining? Did I smile at the waitress? Was I alone?

I remembered nothing.

I didn't remember how I felt.

How the waffles made me feel.

Was I happy, sad, or just still?

Maybe it was one of those rare afternoons where the noise inside me had quietened without asking for explanation.

No dread. No hurry. No ache for something more.

And I think that's why I kept the docket.

Not for the waffles.

But for the moment I didn't realise I was okay.

We never mark those moments properly. We celebrate birthdays and promotions and anniversaries. But no one throws a party for Tuesday at 1:04 pm, when I felt strangely at peace.

So we tuck the receipt into our coat pocket.

Fold it. Forget it.

Until it finds us again and says: "Look. You were here. And it wasn't awful."

I should write something for the small moments.

The overlooked ones.

The gentle, unglamorous pauses in a life.

I screenshotted the receipt and wrote beneath it:

> *You didn't need to be more than you were.*
>
> *And neither did I.*

TWO EURO CANDLES

Chapter 43

My Tears Could Drown It

It started with the smell.

Warm, strange. Like burnt sugar on a stove. Not quite caramel. Not quite ash. Sweet and ruined at the same time.

I sniffed the air and looked around. Nothing out of place. No incense. No spilt candle wax. Just that odd, lingering scent that made the back of my throat tighten.

She came in quietly—late twenties, scarf tied too tightly, hands clutched around a shopping bag like it might bite her.

She walked straight to Mary. Didn't light a candle. Didn't cross herself.

Instead, she opened the bag. Gently, like it held something alive.

Inside: a tiny handmade knitted jumper.

She placed it at Mary's feet and arranged it carefully. Then stood back.

Then said, "I'm sorry. He couldn't be saved."

The church held its breath.

She didn't cry. Just closed her red eyes, lips shaking, no sound.

And that smell—stronger now—seemed to wrap around the whole front of the church like a memory turning bitter at the edges.

Thérèse didn't say anything. Still absent. Or maybe just quiet on purpose.

I stayed seated. Watched. Waited.

The woman stood there for maybe five minutes. Then she leaned in and placed her hand on the base of the mosaic. Once. Soft. Final.

She left the bag behind.

When she turned to leave, her face looked—hollow, yes—but also softer. Like the sharpest edges had dulled.

After she was gone, I walked up to the statue. Looked down.

A note was tucked into the jumper. Folded. Faded.

It read: You made me a mother. Even if only for a little while.

That was it.

Impactful and authentic.

I didn't touch it. Just stood there, hands in my pockets, the smell still thick in my chest.

I didn't touch the tiny jumper. My tears could drown it.

I didn't dance with my emotions, observing was enough.

I was back 1993. In the Belgian Ardennes.

My wife and I lost a child during pregnancy. It was nobody's fault. It was nature doing the right thing, I suppose.

For us, it was torture—a silent one—I didn't know how to handle the situation.

The grief and pain were immense—matching the size of my inadequacy.

I had no clue how to deal with myself, my wife, and our loss.

I didn't offer words of comfort—just plain, painful silence.

Our arms were embracing—our love was simply red eyes and heavy tears.

A harsh milestone for our relationship.

Weeks of humility.

Months of sadness.

Years of unforgiveness.

Grief is funny.

It can smell awful. It can sound like nothing. It can walk into a church and rearrange the air without saying a word. And it's able to flip you upside down without care.

Before I left, I lit a candle for my boy who didn't see the light of life. And for my wife's golden heart.

Chapter 44

I Miss The Sound Of Her

It had been a week. Maybe more.

Still no Thérèse.

No comments. No muttered jokes. No quiet nudges in the back of my head when someone lit a candle upside down. Nothing.

I sat in my usual chair most mornings, phone unlocked, pages mostly blank, no words to contemplate. My fingers lay across the keyboard, waiting for permission to move.

I started writing to her.

Not prayers. Just notes. Letters. If I were writing on old-fashioned paper, I would have left them under the pew like offerings. Some were full of questions. Others, just one line:

Where are you?

No reply.

I read back over the previous entries logged in my Google account. The ones where her voice had danced, teased, challenged, comforted, and observed.

They didn't read like madness. They read like conversations I'd needed. Still needed.

One morning, I tried to force it. Sat in silence, focused hard, whispered her name a dozen times.

Still nothing.

Thérèse, if you're reading this, I wrote,

> *I get it. You're teaching me something. But honestly, this lesson's a bit shit.*

That made me laugh. A little.

Later that afternoon, a nun I'd never seen before passed me near the candle holder. Short, elderly, eyes bright like she knew all the good secrets.

She looked straight at me and said, "She hasn't left you."

"Sorry?"

She just smiled, like we'd already had the conversation, and walked on.

I sat there a long time after that.

I didn't hear a voice. Didn't get a sign.

But when I stood to leave, I contemplated deleting all my Ostend journal entries, but instead I wrote:

Abundance and scarcity.

Is there scarcity in abundance and abundance in scarcity?

Is there a happy medium? Something that doesn't hurt our heart so much.

Should I embrace Thérèse's scarcity as a form of abundance?

Holidaying in Ostend is full of mental challenges—and existential questions.

My awareness is pushing me to accept that I am universally receiving what I should receive.

What was I born to receive—to experience?

The good, the bad, and the ugly are forms of ultimate abundance.

So, what is it that drives me mad about Thérèse's absence?

Is it her motherly love that I am missing?

If so, does she love me the way I want to be loved?

Is that the reason why I feel so scarce in her missing presence?

Maybe I should unlearn the way I love or receive love to appreciate the abundance in my scarcity.

Maybe I should silence my mind and simply appreciate how

the Holy Spirit's love is, has been, and will always be dancing with me or through me.

What will it take to appreciate its gratuitous fullness?

What are my limitations?

What does it take to accept the good, the bad, and the ugly equally?

What is the trade-off?

Or is it just labelled life experiences that need to be emotionally unlabelled?

Is that the simplest way to be—to live?

Is monitoring my emotional content simply peeling the labels off my chaotic life's dance moves?

Is that the way to reach the boundaries of my endless presence—my universal identity?

The church is closing. I have been invited to come back later.

I turned to Thérèse and said, "I miss the sound of you."

Chapter 45

Purple Rain

I heard it first in a bakery.

Soft. Faint. From the radio behind the counter—just a chorus I remembered from sometime in my early twenties. I didn't think much of it, even though it can trigger me emotionally very easily.

Then, later that day, at a pharmacy—there it was again.

Same song. Same wholesome chorus. As if someone had queued it up to haunt me.

I laughed it off. Coincidence. Nothing more.

But that evening, walking back from the train station, a busker was singing it.

Guitar out of tune. Voice like someone who'd lived too hard

too early. But unmistakable.

I froze.

Because now I was listening.

Not just hearing, but listening.

"Purple Rain" was on repeat.

The lyrics were profound. A spiritual manifesto. A restless feeling. A simple story of someone being transcended.

And suddenly I was twenty again, sitting in my white Ford Fiesta on a road trip with someone I never quite loved enough, humming that same song playing on repeat to keep the silence between us from breaking us apart.

I hadn't thought about that day in years.

But the song knew.

The song remembered.

That's the thing about music—it files things away without permission. Locks grief into melody. Binds memory to chord. Then one day it plays again, and you're ambushed.

I stood in front of the busker until he finished.

Dropped a ten-euro note in his case and nodded.

He nodded back, as if he knew exactly what he'd done.

Later, in the flat, I looked up the lyrics properly.

And without knowing, I was transported back to the 21st of April 2016. I was driving a rental Fiat Punto through Germany, heading towards Lausanne. That day, the song played on repeat on the radio. Tears were also on the autobahn when I learned of Prince's passing.

The German Alps were the sanctuary of my mental breakdown.

A serious one. A needed one. A wild one.

I stopped the car at a petrol station on the side of the autobahn and cried my heart into the grass.

It took time for the beauty of the mountains to pull me back to earth.

I was far gone.

How could she forget the worst day of our life?

The grass grounded me slowly.

Betrayal and condescension are my enemies.

I dreamt of being washed by the Purple Rain.

My romantic and melancholic weakness had no power to sit me behind the steering wheel.

The green grass was God's safety blanket, made of faith and hope.

Here in Ostend, in my Airbnb, I didn't cry. I took a series of long breaths, questioning my next best emotional move.

I just sat on the floor, legs crossed like I was in detention. On YouTube, I typed 'Purple Rain' into the search bar and waited for the guitar solo and the angelic voices of the chorus singers to do their holy business.

I felt blessed and at peace.

After the video clip finished, I wrote:

I have a restless attitude to life.

I should have the same attitude to let go of the past.

Chapter 46

She Never Spoke To Me

She started turning up at three o'clock on the dot.

Every day. Same habit. Same seat. Same routine.

She never looked around. Never nodded. Never prayed out loud.

She'd walk straight to the third chair on the left—four rows behind the mosaic—kneel for exactly thirty-three minutes, then rise and leave without a word.

Didn't carry a rosary. Didn't cross herself. Just sat there with a stillness that made the rest of us feel fidgety.

She had the sort of silence that didn't just fill a space—it rearranged it.

One afternoon, I left a folded note on the pew before she

arrived. Just a scribble:

Why do you come?

She never acknowledged it.

But the next day, she left something behind. A torn scrap of paper, neatly folded.

I opened it after she left. Six words, handwritten in tight, slanted script:

Everything blooms underground before it rises.

I didn't know what to do with that. So I folded it again, slipped it into my jacket, and said nothing.

Thérèse still wasn't speaking.

I started to think the nun was her echo. Or her stand-in. Or maybe just a quiet witness meant to keep me from drifting.

Some days she stayed longer than thirty-three minutes. Once she sat for over an hour. Eyes closed. Face unreadable.

She never looked at me. Not once.

But I started sitting in the pew behind her. Not to bother her. Just to be near someone who knew how to sit with the holy in absolute silence.

It became part of my rhythm.

Three o'clock. The nun arrives. The church shifts.

Stillness grows roots.

And something inside me begins to settle.

Strangely, I saw her later walking the streets of Ostend.

She walked past me like I wasn't there.

Black coat, sturdy shoes, weathered face carved from patience. She was clearly not the soft-smiling kind from postcards, but the tough, quiet kind who'd survived war zones and parish meetings with equal grit.

I was standing near the fish market, trying to work out my plan for afternoon tea. Caruso or Caruso?

She caught my eye—briefly. Long enough for me to nod, maybe even smile.

She looked right through me.

Not around me.

Through.

As if I were fog, a streetlight, or a question she had no time for.

It hit harder than I cared to admit.

I stood there, awkward, holding my phone like a shield.

I'd been seen by strangers here, hugged by the mistaken, smiled at by children. But her look—or lack of it—was surgical.

No cruelty.

Just absence.

Like Thérèse.

I told myself maybe she was tired. Maybe she was deep in prayer. Maybe she just didn't want to be bothered by some tourist wearing spiritual uncertainty.

But it didn't matter.

The damage had been done.

Later, sitting on a bench with a greasy paper cone of frites, I tried to laugh it off.

I didn't need approval from a passing nun. I didn't need her approval.

But the sting lingered.

And I realised it wasn't about her.

It was about me.

Still wanting to be noticed.

Validated.

Named.

Even here.

Even now.

Even by someone whose entire vocation might be about not being impressed by the surface of things.

I stayed seated a little bit longer.

Just breathed.

And thought—what if it's okay to be invisible sometimes?

What if I didn't need to be welcomed, forgiven, adored, or understood?

What if the point isn't to be seen, but to keep showing up anyway?

Then I stopped and recalled Thérèse's voice saying: "Keep showing up, even when it's boring."

TWO EURO CANDLES

Chapter 47

The Secrets We Don't Pray Aloud

It was market day. Quiet. Raining lightly outside, the sort that soaks your sleeves without ever turning into a proper downpour.

Inside, a man in his forties sat up front, lips moving—but no sound came out. Not even a whisper. Just the shape of prayer without the voice.

I couldn't look away.

He finished, crossed himself with care, and walked out like someone leaving a confessional with all the real stuff still locked inside.

Thérèse once said: "The things we don't say are loudest in heaven."

I was beginning to understand what she meant.

A woman entered next. Lit her candle. Looked around nervously. Then made the sign of the cross seventeen times—fast, frantic, like she was trying to erase something from her soul. She left without kneeling. But her flame lingered.

Then a child, maybe nine, walked in with his grandad. He held a folded piece of paper like it was treasure. Without speaking, he tucked it into the purple curtain next to Mary.

After they were gone, I peeked. The note was written in thick pencil:

> *Mum and Dad, are you in heaven?*
>
> *When are you coming back?*
>
> *I love you.*
>
> *Brent.*

I sat down. Hard.

Didn't move for a while.

It struck me then—how many people came here not to pray out loud, but to smuggle their hope in quietly, like contraband.

They didn't ask for flashy miracles. They just wanted not to be alone with the ache anymore.

I fit the profile perfectly.

I didn't light a candle.

I didn't ask anything out loud.

I just sat.

And in the quiet that followed, I swear I heard breathing—not mine, not anyone else's. Just the sound of presence.

The church isn't empty when no one speaks.

It's full of what we're too afraid—or too tender—to say.

TWO EURO CANDLES

Chapter 48

To Dad

And so today, I wrote him a letter.

Not because I think he can read it.

Not because I need a reply.

But because it's time for me to let go and trust the universal recycling facility.

I wrote a letter to my dad. He won't read it. I won't mail it.

> *Dear Dad,*
>
> *You were wrong about a lot of things.*
>
> *And so was I.*
>
> *But I think we both loved each other underneath it.*

I displayed my affection.

You affirmed strictness.

You wanted discipline.

I wanted softness.

You spoke in tasks.

I spoke in escape routes.

You raised me through hard, tight fists and harsh insults.

I ran away.

And neither of us knew how to meet in the middle without it looking like surrender.

But I saw you.

I saw the way you checked the oil in my car, even when we weren't speaking.

I saw the way you stayed up until I got home, pretending to read.

I saw how you looked at Mum when she laughed and didn't know it.

I saw you holding our kid's hand while crossing the road.

I saw you trying.

And I want you to know—I'm trying too.

Not to become you.

But to carry what was good about you into something gentler.

I love you.

Even if we never got the words right.

And I love you.

For the life experience you gave me.

Love,

Your son.

Maxsense

I folded the letter. Placed it in my suitcase.

That night, I lit two candles.

One for him.

One for who I'm still becoming.

TWO EURO CANDLES

Chapter 49

The Return of the Flower

At the first hour of the morning, I ran and sat, committed to confessing to Mary, God, and the Universe.

Like the little boy the other day, I came prepared. I had printed my confession list.

As there was nowhere for me to escape anymore, I committed:

> *I confess I am still unsettled about being raised with domestic violence, and verbal and physical abuse at home.*
>
> *I confess I am still unsettled about being raised with mental punishment at home.*
>
> *I confess that I hated my parents' controlling and diminishing behaviours.*
>
> *I confess I hate my father for beating my mother when I was young.*

I confess that I didn't like it when my father put a loaded gun to my head.

I confess that I didn't like it when my father fired his gun in the house.

I confess that I did not like it when my father beat me for no reason.

I confess that I did not like my father for strangling my sister over a bad boyfriend choice.

I confess that throughout my whole youth I wished my father would die.

I confess that I hate my parents for rewriting their life story and pretending to be goody-goody people.

I confess that I hate how my parents interpret historical events.

I confess that my parents don't take ownership of their bullshit.

I confess that my parents don't take ownership of their mental poverty.

I confess that my parents' inner children are suffering.

I confess that I understand human weakness.

I confess that I experienced human weakness—including mine.

I confess that I never understood how a grown man could demolish a brand-new dishwasher he'd just purchased.

I confess that I never comprehended why my father was kicking holes in the doors we had just installed throughout the house.

I confess that being a passenger was frightening when my father—while driving—savagely destroyed the manual gearbox of a car he could barely afford.

I confess that seeing my father flip the dining table full of food before a meal was scary.

I confess that seeing my father shoot a dog in the family courtyard in broad daylight was disturbing.

I confess that seeing my father rip the old phone line off the wall was intimidating.

I confess that my father being a cop gave him the upper hand over his family. Help wasn't available.

I confess that my father had a habit of slapping me in the face before dropping me at school when my way of saying goodbye didn't meet his standards.

I confess that I hate my father questioning my sexuality because I made a friend who didn't care that I was the son of the sheriff.

I confess that I hate the way my father would trap me or my siblings in a kitchen corner by pushing the kitchen table towards us.

I confess that on the day I ran away from home, my father tried to beat me again. This time, knowing my life was in danger, I was the first to move the kitchen table. He stumbled backwards and looked foolish. A few moments later, he tried to take his own life—attempting to hang himself out the back of the garage. Before I left, without knowing why, I went to check on him and cut the rope.

I confess that I worry about my brother committing suicide.

I confess that I worry about my brother talking about death and not life.

I confess that it breaks my heart that my siblings aren't talking to each other.

I confess that it breaks my heart that my siblings judge each other wrongly.

I confess that I don't enjoy seeing my family apart.

I confess that I worry about my sisters' mental states.

I confess that I lost trust in my mother when she read my girlfriend's love letters and started blackmailing me.

I confess that I have problems accepting the damage done by my father to our family.

I confess that my father destroyed my siblings' emotional wellbeing and their love lives.

I confess that my father was racist and restricted my sisters from having exotic boyfriends.

I confess that if throwing shoes at your children to hurt them were a sport, my father would have been a gold medallist for ten years in a row.

I confess that I feel pain not knowing my parents outside their reactive behaviour.

I confess that I ran away from Belgium to raise my family in a haven.

I confess that sometimes I am lost emotionally.

I confess that sadness and emptiness visit me far too frequently.

I confess that I am smart but sabotage myself often.

I confess that my emotional life is sometimes a burden.

I confess that my reactive behaviour is my downfall.

I confess that I am question my life direction and choices.

I confess that my voice is sometimes muffled.

I confess that I am relieved to know the paedophile who raped and sexually abused me is dead.

I confess that I love every woman who ever formed my love life.

I confess that I stopped loving every woman who tried to control me.

I confess that I did not like it when my father did not acknowledge my son when they met for the first time.

I confess that I dreamt of bloody revenge towards my father for a big part of my life.

I confess that I doubt myself sometimes.

I confess that I believe in miracles.

I confess that miracles happen.

I confess I am a miracle receiver.

I confess that I believe in God but I am not a religious person.

I confess that I am not happy with the first and middle names I received.

I confess that as a novelist I use a pen name to honour my mum's wishes.

I confess that there was joy in my upbringing, but the colours of domestic violence, and verbal and physical abuse, made it hard to enjoy or recall.

I confess that my emotional baggage did not make me a good boyfriend.

I confess that people saw or judged me as the cop's son and not for who I am.

I confess that my father attempted suicide twice.

I confess that as much as I hated my father as a teenager, I did not want him to die when he had a bad car accident.

I confess that most of my life I have blamed my parents for my situation and failures.

I confess that emotional and spiritual freedom are the upside of my upbringing.

I confess that diminishing words are harder to process than hard punches.

I confess that I was more scared of my father's reactive behaviour than of being raped.

I confess that I was hurt when I was told to refrain from expressing my pain during a kundalini session.

I confess that I studied and practised architecture to prove to my father that I am not an idiot.

I confess that I have little pleasure in being an architect.

I confess that I have no interest in designing my own house.

I confess that everything I design, write or paint feels old as soon as it is completed.

I confess that I have a need for ongoing learning, rebirth, and spiritual awareness.

I confess that I am restless and will not settle for the status quo.

I confess that it was hard to stop being a perfectionist.

I confess that I can only count on myself.

I confess that I did not like it when my father told me I was good for nothing.

I confess that I did not enjoy being called a clown by my father.

I confess that I did not enjoy being called a bastard by my mum.

I confess that I did not appreciate being bullied at school.

I confess that being bashed at school was not fun.

I confess that I dreamt of bloody revenge towards my school bullies.

I confess it was challenging to face one of my school bullies when I was last in Belgium.

I confess that I lie to get by.

I confess that I lie to have a better emotional life.

I confess that I lie to survive.

I confess that I experienced full body enlightenment once.

I confess that my work as a hypnotist with cancer patients has not been easy emotionally.

I confess that my first true adult relationship breakdown was bloody painful.

I confess that I did not like my first true adult relationship being marred by violence, control and insecurity.

I confess that I was unaware of my reactive behaviours for most of my life.

I confess that I have a learning addiction because my father told me I was worthless.

I confess that at times I have pushed my negative emotional agenda.

I confess that I spent a big part of my life doing things to seek my father's recognition and failed miserably.

I confess that I spent a big part of my life doing instead of being, only to achieve nothing in the end.

I confess I seek emotional refuge in my work.

I confess that I am frustrated by not having genuine conversations with my parents.

I confess that I am not looking forward to the passing of my parents.

I confess that I am the black sheep of the family.

I confess that I have the freedom to feel, smell, touch, see, and hear all day long.

I confess that I sucked at relationships at an early age.

I confess that I have felt lonely for a big part of my life.

I confess that I have difficulty committing to long-term ventures.

I confess that I am scared to take out a mortgage and make long-term commitments.

I confess that I didn't always make the best decisions in my business.

I confess that I was ignorant as a young business owner.

I confess that I am scared of not being paid for my work.

I confess that I have had difficult financial experiences with clients.

I confess that I am scared of being broke.

I confess that I am scared of not being able to provide for my loved ones.

I confess that I became self-employed to do the opposite of my father.

I confess that I had poor money management for years.

I confess that I am a privileged person regardless of the money I make.

I confess that Franco's creative sexual education has served me well throughout my life.

I confess that Louis' craftsmanship mentoring has helped me land on my feet numerous times.

I confess that Bruna's emotional and self-healing lessons have been converted into a way of living.

I confess that sometimes anxiety creeps up on me from nowhere.

I confess that I have a beautiful life.

I confess that I am no victim after all.

I stopped reading, folded the paper back into my jacket, and took a long, deep breath.

The church was quiet.

Mary was still glazed ceramic.

The statue of Thérèse was still plaster and wood.

And then out of nowhere, I heard her laugh before I heard her words.

Not loudly. Not even out loud. Just there, tucked inside the stillness like a breeze slipping under the door.

"Well," Thérèse said. "You've been dramatic."

I nearly fainted. My heart did something awkward in my chest—half skip, half stumble.

"You're back," I whispered.

"Don't call it a comeback," she teased. "I never left. You just got quiet enough to miss me."

I exhaled like someone who'd been holding their breath for a week and a half.

"You left me in the dark," I muttered, which sounded more petulant than I meant.

"And yet," she said, "you stayed and committed."

I couldn't argue with that.

She let the silence stretch a moment before speaking again. "You've grown, you know. In that slow, garden-bed kind of way."

"I'm not sure I've grown. I think I've just broken better."

"That's still growth," she said. "Cracks are how the light gets permission."

I closed my eyes and let her voice fill the spaces where loneliness had started to settle in.

I told her everything. Quietly. The doubts. The frustration. The weird moments. The unspoken prayer I'd folded into the pew.

She didn't interrupt. Didn't solve anything. Just listened like the whole universe had been waiting for me to say exactly what I'd just said.

When I was finished, I asked, "Why now? Why come back today?"

She smiled—I could feel it more than hear it.

"Because you're not looking for signs anymore. You're just here. And that's where miracles like to live."

Before I left, I lit a candle. No request. No condition. Just thanks.

And as I turned to go, I noticed something.

A single white rose, resting on my chair. No note. No explanation. Just waiting.

She didn't say it was from her.

She didn't need to.

Chapter 50

I Didn't Want To Wake Up

It wasn't dramatic.

No weeping. No whispered pleas. No great existential howl into the mattress.

Just a dull thud in the chest. A tiredness that had calcified overnight. I opened my eyes, saw the ceiling of the little flat, and thought: No. Not yet.

There was nothing wrong. Not exactly.

I hadn't lost a job. No phone call with bad news. No fight. No heartbreak.

Just life. Quiet, undisturbed, and unbearably heavy.

Some days arrive like that—uninvited. They sit on your chest like a coat you forgot you were still wearing, and you wonder how long you'll keep going before something snaps.

I didn't get up for an hour.

Just lay there, cocooned in the doona, the kettle unboiled, the light creeping under the curtains like a trespasser.

I wasn't sad. I wasn't anxious.

I just… didn't want to.

Didn't want to shower. Didn't want to think. Didn't want to open my Word files that had so far forgiven everything I'd thrown at them.

Eventually, I rolled out of bed and put on my newly acquired hoodie.

The street was grey. The coffee was okay. The barista didn't look up when I paid.

And still—here I was.

Alive.

Which felt like both a triumph and a joke.

I sat in the park with a paper cup, watching pigeons fight over nothing. A child screamed with joy near the fountain. Someone sneezed so loudly it made a group of tourists laugh.

And I thought—This. This is what I would've missed.

Not the big things.

Not the fireworks.

But the tiny, absurd, beautiful reminders that the world doesn't need me to feel worthy in order to keep offering me small graces.

That afternoon, I walked into the church and sat at the very back.

Didn't pray. Didn't cry.

Just sat. Quiet. Alive.

Still not entirely sure that I wanted to be—but choosing it anyway.

I lit a candle.

Watched the flame flicker like it was trying to decide whether to stay.

TWO EURO CANDLES

Chapter 51

We Are All Cracked Vessels

That morning, I didn't record any of my experiences on my phone.

I don't know why. I think I was tired of documenting every flicker, every whisper, every shift in the atmosphere. I just wanted to be there. No analysis. No scribbles. Just breath and bones and whatever faith had become for me now.

Thérèse arrived before I even sat down.

"Ready?" she asked.

"For what?"

"For the part where you stop pretending your past doesn't matter."

I sighed. Sat. Rested my hands on my thighs like I was trying to camouflage a confession to someone who already knew.

"I've wasted time," I said.

"Everyone does."

"I let people down."

"So has every saint worth remembering."

"I've lied."

"Haven't we all."

I swallowed. "There was someone I should've loved better. Years ago. I still think about her."

Thérèse didn't flinch. "Then light a candle for her. But also light one for the version of you that couldn't love properly back then."

I blinked.

"You want a miracle?" she said. "Here it is: you can name what you regret and not be ruined by it."

I sat with that. Long enough to feel something shift.

"I thought saints were meant to fix us," I said quietly.

She laughed. "Saints aren't mechanics. We just sit with you until you remember you're not broken—just poured through."

"Poured through?"

"Like clay. Like glass. Like anything that was made to hold

light."

The candles burned brighter that day. Or maybe I just noticed them differently.

Before I left, I lit two flames.

One for her.

One for me.

Neither of us perfect. Both of us worthy.

Afterwards, my head needed a break.

I needed clarity in my headspace.

Middelkerke was the destination. So, I jumped on the tram.

It was a full carriage—midday, midweek, packed with backpacks and elbows and perfume that tried too hard.

I was standing near the back, one hand clutching the overhead rail, the other holding a plastic bag with a sandwich I didn't really want. My shoulders ached from nothing specific. Just life.

She was sitting near the middle—an older woman, scarf tied with purpose, groceries in a neat cloth bag at her feet. She didn't glance up. Just saw me in the reflection, maybe. Or felt the shift in the air. Or read the slump in my spine like a headline.

And without saying a word, she stood.

Stepped aside. Gestured.

Didn't smile. Didn't insist. Didn't offer me a noble moment.

Just… moved.

I sat down, awkward, grateful, embarrassed in that stubborn way we sometimes are when someone sees our tiredness before we're ready to admit to it.

"Thank you," I said.

She didn't reply.

Just adjusted her scarf, grabbed a handrail, and stared out the window like it was her job.

I watched her the rest of the ride. She got off two stops later. Didn't look back. Was swallowed by the footpath crowd like she'd never existed at all.

But I remembered.

I still do.

Because sometimes kindness is loud.

But sometimes it's stealthy.

A quiet realignment of space that says: "You look like you need this more than I do. And I'm not keeping score."

That afternoon, I didn't do much.

Just walked. Ate the sandwich slowly. Wrote a few lines on my phone.

And for a moment,

I felt human again.

That evening, I lit a candle.

Not for her exactly. I didn't know her name.

But for the gesture. The grace. The everyday holiness that passes between strangers in crowded spaces.

TWO EURO CANDLES

Chapter 52

You Are The Miracles

A man sat down beside me. Middle-aged. Nervous hands. Eyes like someone searching for the right sentence in a language he'd forgotten how to speak.

He leaned over and asked, "What do I pray for?"

I paused.

Not because I didn't know what to say—but because I finally did.

"Something small," I told him. "Something real. Something that doesn't sound like a slogan."

He nodded slowly, then whispered, "Like what?"

I looked around. Candles flickering. The soft groan of the old timber pews. The silence that somehow felt warmer now than it used to.

I said, "Pray to be the kind of person a miracle would visit."

His eyes welled up. Just a bit. He gave a nod—not to me, but to Mary.

Then he stood, lit a candle, and didn't say a word.

I watched him walk out into the grey light. No lightning bolt. No holy music. Just a man a little less afraid of his own softness.

Thérèse whispered, "Look at you."

I smiled. "What?"

"You're doing it."

"Doing what?"

"Being part of it. You stopped spectating. You joined the story."

I looked down at my hands, still folded without even realising. Still.

It didn't feel like I'd changed the world. But something inside had finally stopped pacing.

"I don't feel like a miracle," I said.

"No one does," she replied. "But it doesn't stop it being true."

The candle the man had lit flared as he left. A sharp flicker. Then calm.

I stayed behind for a while, just sitting.

Not needing proof.

Not needing words.

Just being there.

Like that was enough.

Thérèse's words invited me back to the library. I needed to read her letters again. I needed validation in my understanding—ticking boxes on miracles terminology.

Or simply ticking boxes on my realisation.

The library wasn't very helpful. I couldn't read Flemish. I tried my luck somewhere else—a second-hand bookstore.

The man behind the counter asked, "You on holiday or working?"

And I said, "Working."

Straight face. Steady voice. Eyes on the till. Just a reflex.

He nodded. Handed me my change. No follow-up questions. No quiz.

But I felt it—hot and immediate—the sting of having betrayed myself for absolutely no reason.

Why did I say that?

Why did I lie?

It wasn't a lie that mattered.

It didn't hurt anyone.

Didn't ruin a reputation.

Didn't involve stolen cash or broken trust or borrowed hearts.

But it sat there in my chest all afternoon like a small rock in my shoe.

It wasn't the words.

It was the reason behind them.

I didn't want to admit I was on holiday because it sounded… aimless.

Like I had too much time.

Like I wasn't useful.

Like I was just wandering.

Which, of course, is exactly what I am.

And for a moment, I was ashamed of it.

Ashamed of being someone who takes up space without a business card or deadline or productivity metric attached.

So I lied.

And then hated the lie.

It made me wonder how many other times I've smoothed over the truth—not to deceive, but to self-protect. How often I've made myself smaller, simpler, more digestible in the name of convenience.

That evening, I walked back to the bookshop. Didn't go in. Just stood across the road, watching through the window.

He was still there. Stamping the back pages of new donations. Quiet, ordinary, kind-looking.

I thought about going in. Saying something like:

"Actually, I lied. I'm not working. I'm on a break. I'm in the middle of a soft collapse. But thanks for not prying."

I didn't, of course.

But I whispered it anyway. I didn't want to succumb any longer to my "to do" demons and simply wanted to embrace the godly invite of being.

Standing on the kerb, I realised that I was not a kid anymore who needed to lie to survive or to hide unpleasant truths.

Thérèse once said: There is nothing wrong with me. And there never was.

So, why did I sabotage my pleasure at being in Ostend?

Her words about making a fountain of youth out of our life experience suddenly resonated within me.

They knocked me hard in the centre of my chest.

It all starts with the little things that build the foundation of your integrity.

That night, I wrote:

I told a lie so small it hurt.

Because the truth felt too unremarkable.

But maybe being unremarkable

is exactly what I'm learning to carry.

Gently.

Proudly.

Honestly.

Chapter 53

Cleaning The Candle Display

I started wiping down the candle racks.

No one asked me to. No one paid me. I just showed up one morning with a cloth and a pocket knife and decided the melted wax had built up enough to justify some gentle intervention.

The black steel stand had grown crusty with weeks—maybe years—of prayers gone molten. I scraped and wiped, polished and buffed. It felt oddly satisfying.

"Look at you," Thérèse said. "Saint of tidying."

"Someone's got to do it."

"Exactly. That's the secret."

The tourists ignored me. They always do. They probably

assumed I was some sort of part-time maintenance guy or underpaid sacristan. One lady even asked me where the toilets were.

I just nodded towards the corridor and said, "Follow the scent of detergent and divine resignation."

Some of the old wax peeled off in satisfying strips. A few coins had melted themselves into crevices, like stubborn little blessings refusing to let go.

As I worked, I found something wedged behind the lowest row of candle cups—a scrap of paper.

Faded. Slightly burnt at one corner. Just four words: "Make me soft again."

I stared at it for a while. Folded it up. Put it in my pocket.

It felt like someone else's prayer that had been waiting for me to find it.

By the time I finished cleaning, my back was tight—but something inside me was strangely loose. Like the kind of tired you earn.

One of the priests passed by and gave me a thumbs up.

"Good work," he said.

I shrugged. "Just cleaning wax."

He winked. "That's where most of the real holiness hides."

Thérèse whispered, "Now you're starting to get it."

And for the first time, I wasn't searching for miracles.

I was helping prepare a place for them.

TWO EURO CANDLES

Chapter 54

Ten Years Ago, I Was Her

She was sitting on the bench across from the carousel—legs crossed, coat too thin for the wind, hair scraped back like she'd stopped bothering to impress anyone. Face hidden behind a dog-eared notebook. Pen moving fast.

I saw her from a distance and froze.

Because for a second, I could've sworn it was me.

Not literally, of course.

But something about the posture. The restless way she chewed the end of the pen cap. The frayed sleeve of a jumper that had seen too many breakdowns and not enough rest days. The way she kept looking up and then pretending not to care what anyone else was doing.

I knew that version of myself.

Ten years ago, I was her.

Writing to stay sane.

Journalling instead of speaking.

Wearing shoes with soles that had outlived their purpose.

Pockets full of travel receipts, tension, and crumbs.

I sat on the bench opposite her.

Not to stare.

Just to remember.

She didn't notice me.

Or maybe she did, and decided not to.

She tore a page from her notebook. Crumpled it. Missed the bin. Didn't bother trying again.

And I remembered how much I used to do that—write something too raw, too close to true, then bin it like my feelings were recyclable.

I wanted to go over.

Hand her a coffee.

Tell her she's not broken, just overwhelmed.

That the things she's writing down now will make sense someday.

That she's not alone.

That healing isn't linear.

That rest is not failure.

But I didn't.

Because I wouldn't have believed any of that at her age either.

So I stayed where I was.

Let her have her bench, her page, her silence.

And instead, I whispered it into the wind.

Just loud enough that maybe the version of me still stuck in that decade could hear it.

That evening, I went to the church and lit a candle.

This time, I imagined placing it into the hands of my younger self.

Told him quietly, "You don't need to figure it all out. Just stay. Just write. Just breathe."

TWO EURO CANDLES

Chapter 55

Prayer Without Panic

She entered without ceremony.

No rushing. No fumbling. No whispered rehearsals under her breath. Just walked in, calm as morning light, and sat two pews behind the candle rack.

Late fifties, maybe older. Cardigan. Neat hair. A face you'd forget instantly unless you paid proper attention—which, for once, I did.

She didn't light a candle. Didn't cross herself.

She just... sat. Hands open on her lap. Eyes closed. Breathing slow and steady, like she was somewhere safer than the rest of us knew how to be.

I kept waiting for her to move. For a gesture. A glance. A

sign she was doing something more than sitting there like a cushion with a pulse.

But she didn't.

Thérèse spoke gently. "That's how it's meant to look."

"What is?"

"Prayer without panic."

I watched her for seventeen minutes. She didn't twitch. Didn't check her watch. Didn't bargain with God or list her grievances.

And when she finally opened her eyes, she smiled—not at Mary, not at heaven, not at anything in particular.

Just smiled.

Then got up, nodded to no one, and walked out.

That was it.

No miracle. No mystery. Just stillness.

But the stillness changed the room. Or maybe just changed me.

"She didn't ask for anything," I said.

"She didn't have to," Thérèse replied. "Sometimes, presence is the whole point."

I stayed behind, trying to copy her posture. Hands open. No script.

It felt awkward at first. Then strange. Then peaceful.

I didn't ask for anything either.

And for once, I didn't feel like I was missing out.

TWO EURO CANDLES

Chapter 56

He Gave Me a Wink

It was the wink that did me in.

Not the art. Not the dramatic lighting or the near-religious silence in the halls. Just that one small, knowing flick of the eye from a man in a navy-blue waistcoat who clearly took more joy in people than in paintings.

I was in the Ensor House.

Not because I'm cultured—but because it was drizzling, and I needed somewhere to stand still without explaining myself.

I wandered past crooked masks, ghostly self-portraits, skeletons in fancy hats. James Ensor had a way of painting the madness under politeness. It felt familiar.

I lingered in a corner room, staring too long at a work I didn't quite understand. Something about it unsettled me—figures with faces that smirked too wide, joy laced with teeth.

Then I felt him behind me.

The guide. Older man. Sharp eyes. Wrists like coat hangers. The kind of bloke who could spot a lost soul from across the parquet floor.

He didn't say a word.

Just gave me the tiniest nod. Then, as he turned to walk away, a wink.

Cheeky. Light. Like he'd just let me in on a secret no one else in the room would get.

And I don't know why, but I nearly burst into tears.

Not because of the wink, really.

Because someone saw me.

Not as a tourist.

Not as a loner.

Just... as a person.

Standing in front of a painting, trying not to fall apart.

I left the museum quietly.

Stood outside under the awning and let the rain mist my face.

The wink stayed with me all day.

Later, at the church, I sat in a pew and thought about all the ways people hold each other together without knowing it.

A look. A gesture. A kindness slipped into a moment like a folded note in a stranger's coat pocket.

I lit a candle. Not for anything profound.

Just for all the small mercies.

The winks.

The nods.

The gestures that say: I see you. And you're doing alright.

Later, I wrote:

> *Sometimes the real art is the quiet affirmation that you're not invisible.*

TWO EURO CANDLES

Chapter 57

The Choir Boy

He arrived early. Black shoes polished, white shirt tucked in like he'd just been told off about it in the car.

Maybe eleven, maybe twelve. Hair gelled in a way only a parent can manage. Voice still hovering somewhere between child and whatever comes next.

He walked up to the candles with all the seriousness of someone about to sit a test.

Dropped in a coin. Lit one carefully. Bowed his head and whispered:

"Please don't let me squeak on the high note."

I grinned. So did Thérèse.

"Best prayer I've heard all week," she said.

The boy crossed himself, then ran off towards the back of the church where the choir was already gathering. Sheet music rustling. Warm-up coughs. The occasional poorly timed note.

They began with something simple. Latin, soft. Then climbed into the higher register.

And there it was.

Not a squeak—no, more of a wobble. A beautiful, heartbreaking little crack right in the middle of a clear, earnest note.

He didn't flinch.

Just kept singing.

And that crack? It made the song better. More human. More... holy.

When the piece ended, the choir director smiled. Clapped once. The boy looked relieved. Not proud—relieved.

He returned to the candle he'd lit. Stared at it. Then grinned, like he was in on the joke now.

Thérèse whispered, "God prefers the cracks."

"Why?"

"Because they let the light out."

I lit a candle next to his.

Not because I had a high note coming.

But because I wanted to remember that perfection was

never the point.

TWO EURO CANDLES

Chapter 58

I'm Going All In

It arrived on a plate the size of a steering wheel.

Dusted in icing sugar. Half-folded, half-sprawled. Topped with banana slices that were trying to look exotic, modest and failing. A dollop of whipped cream that might've been applied with a shovel.

I stared at it like it had just insulted my ancestors.

The waiter smiled. "Bon appétit."

I nodded, trying to look unbothered.

But inside, I was panicking.

Because this wasn't just a pancake.

It was a commitment.

It was the kind of food that asked: Are you sure you know who you are?

I picked up my fork. Took the first bite.

It was perfect.

Crisp at the edges, soft in the middle, warm like something had gone right in the kitchen and in life, just this once.

I should've stopped halfway.

That would've been sensible. Adult. Measured.

But I didn't.

I kept going like a teenager hungry for mischief.

Because it had been a hard week.

Because my body was tired.

Because I was tired of denying myself things that gave me joy just so I could feel in control.

So I finished it.

All of it.

Right down to the last smug banana slice.

When the plate was cleared, I felt equal parts triumphant and absurd.

Bloated but happy.

Full, not just in the stomach, but in some old, empty corner of myself that had spent too long negotiating with joy.

On the way out, I passed a man looking at the menu outside.

He asked, "Is the pancake worth it?"

I grinned.

"Absolutely."

My grin converted instantly into a text memo for all the ways I've learned to take up space.

To say yes.

To stop halfway through a moment and decide, No, I'm going all in.

TWO EURO CANDLES

Chapter 59

Plastic Raincoat

He shuffled in looking like a bin liner had come to life.

Clear plastic poncho, fogged-up glasses, waterproof camera swinging wildly from his neck. He was drenched from the knees down and squelched with every step.

Everyone turned to look. You couldn't not.

He smiled awkwardly. Said something in broken French— "désolé, il pleut, il mouille"—and sat down right up the front like he'd bought premium tickets to salvation.

"Ah," Thérèse said. "Our lady of lost bookings."

I chuckled. The man fumbled with his camera, wiped his lens, then gave up and just stared at the ceiling.

He didn't light a candle. Didn't cross himself. Just sat there, dripping, trying to catch his breath.

After a while, he pulled out a folded paper map—like it was still 1997—and stared at it with genuine heartbreak.

He muttered something in Dutch. Or German. Or maybe just Touristese.

Then something budged.

He looked up at Mary. Blinked. Stared for a long time.

And then—without fanfare—he took off the poncho. Slowly. Folded it neatly. Wiped his glasses. Dried the corners of his eyes. And smiled.

It wasn't the kind of smile you give when something goes right. It was the kind you give when something lands—inside you.

He walked up to the candle stand. Dug in his coin purse. Lit one. Nodded—not to Mary, not to God. Just... to the air.

Then he left. No photos. No selfie. No souvenir but the wet socks in his shoes.

"Do you think he got what he came for?" I asked.

"Of course not," Thérèse said. "He got something better."

"What's that?"

"A pause."

Outside, the rain eased. Light filtered through the windows like something had loosened above us.

Out of my candle addiction, I lit one too. For everyone wandering into holiness by accident.

Even in plastic.

TWO EURO CANDLES

Chapter 60

The Wild Ones

She didn't say goodbye.

She just said, "You're ready."

I was sitting on my usual chair, watching the light slant differently through the stained glass, when her voice came as soft as breath:

"It's nearly time for me to go."

I froze. "Go where?"

"Nowhere. Just... back into the silence. You'll still hear me. Just not like this."

I wanted to argue. To bargain. To ask for one more miracle, one more clever aside. But I didn't.

Instead, I asked, "What if I forget how to listen?"

She paused.

"Then look for roses," she said. "Not the fancy kind. Not the ones in florist windows. The wild ones. The quiet ones. They'll remind you."

I nodded. Swallowed the lump in my throat.

"And if I see one?"

"Say hello."

That was it.

No final teaching. No curtain call. Just presence, steady and kind, folding back into the corners of the church like incense into air.

I sat there a while longer. Didn't cry. Didn't move.

I opened my wallet and took out the dry rose petal I'd saved a while ago.

I smiled at the memory it offered me and at the present opportunities on offer.

Out of nowhere, "Hello," I whispered.

The candle I'd lit earlier flickered once, then settled into the calmest burn I'd ever seen.

She didn't need to say anything else.

She'd taught me how to notice.

And that was the whole point.

TWO EURO CANDLES

Chapter 61

A Sense Of Urgency

It happened on the corner of a quiet street, just near a waffle stand that smelled like safety and burnt sugar.

She tapped my elbow gently—like you'd tap a biscuit to test its softness. Small frame. Wool beret. Eyes the colour of rinsed-out tea.

"Excuse me," she said in French-accented English, "do you have the time?"

I checked my watch.

"Three twenty-seven," I said, adding a nod, as if to affirm the truth of it.

She smiled, said "Merci," and started walking again. But then paused.

"I don't wear watches anymore," she said, almost to herself. "I find it better not to know."

I smiled politely, unsure if this was an invitation or an ending.

She continued without looking back. Small steps. No urgency.

I stood there a moment too long.

It wasn't just what she said—it was the way she said it. Not like she was whimsical. More like she was telling me something important, and trusting I'd file it away properly.

And I did.

I kept thinking about it all afternoon.

I find it better not to know.

Not to know the time.

Not to know what's coming.

Not to count the hours or the steps or the calories or the days since someone last texted back.

I'd spent my life measuring everything.

Every deadline. Every emotion. Every silence. Every hour. Every reactive behaviour.

But this woman—she'd opted out.

She wasn't resisting time.

She was just refusing to be bullied by it.

Later, sitting near the marina, I watched people check their phones like they were waiting for permission to breathe. I kept my hands in my pockets.

I didn't check the time again that day.

The following day, in the church, I sat on a pew with no intention to rush.

Didn't count the minutes.

Didn't look at the flickering candle as a timer.

Just... sat.

Existed.

Let time be something outside of me.

Breathed deeply, acknowledging that time is not a renewable resource.

Something struck me hard in the chest—like a lightbulb moment.

Had I understood her question properly?

Was she meaning clock time, or was she meaning universal time as an invitation to acknowledge that time is something running out fast?

Was her nonchalance hiding a sense of urgency?

In a panic, I questioned myself.

Do I have time to be me?

To experience life as a holy blessing?

To breathe and act my thoughts into actions, and accept the consequences that come from it?

Chapter 62

A Place Of Respite

Same chair. Same draft. Same black steel candle rack.

Same statue of Mary with her unreadable face and patient hands.

But nothing was the same.

I still came most days. Sometimes early. Sometimes after lunch. Sometimes just long enough to sit down, breathe deeply in the silence, and check if my heart had shifted shape again.

People still came and went. Lighting candles with clumsy hands and desperate hopes. Some still prayed out loud. Some just cried. Some said nothing and left with a little less weight than they brought in.

And me?

I noticed things a little more. Mainly the little things.

A coin left on the floor near the candle box—unspent. A child humming as she lit a flame with her father's help. A cleaner who paused mid-mop to whisper something into the mosaic's ear.

I'd started talking to people too.

Nothing dramatic. Just nods. The occasional "Are you okay?" when someone's shoulders looked too heavy.

I didn't have answers. But I'd learned how to stay.

And that—Thérèse had taught me—was sometimes all a miracle needed.

Someone came in today and sat beside me. Young. Restless. Notebook in hand.

They looked at me and asked, "Is this where people come for help?"

I smiled.

"Sometimes," I said. "Sometimes they just come to remember they're not broken."

They looked confused. I didn't explain.

Instead, I pointed to the candle stand.

"Light one. See what happens."

They did.

And in that moment, I realised something.

I wasn't just watching anymore.

I'd become part of the rhythm—the creak, the hush, the breath between prayers.

All I wanted was to provide a trampoline to the lightness of life.

And Mary watched, same as always.

Only now, I could swear she looked a little amused.

I was a few days away from the end of my stay in Ostend.

At lunch, I was sitting in the conservatory of a seaside café—sunlight filtered through foggy glass, the gentle racket of mugs being stacked and spoons being stirred.

My mind drifted.

It did so with great ease, letting my creative spirit take over. A world without limits, borders, or judgement.

A world for me.

A place of respite.

A book lay open on my lap, but I hadn't turned the page in twenty minutes.

To anyone passing by, I probably looked content. Immersed. Absorbed.

But I wasn't reading.

I was dreaming.

I was in a state of unfocused focus.

I was watching the world creatively.

Not in a creepy way—just... attentively. With that strange kind of focus that comes when the heart is still a little sore and needs something to latch onto without committing.

A young couple sat two tables away. He kept looking at her like he was waiting for the version of her he used to know to come back. She smiled at everything except him.

Near the window, an older man traced the rim of his teacup with one finger over and over, like he was rewriting a memory.

Two teenagers behind me were pretending not to cry-laugh at something on a phone.

And I just sat there, still.

Pretending to read.

Letting myself exist without having to perform usefulness.

Because reading, I've realised, is one of the few public activities that lets you vanish without question.

If you're on your phone, people assume you're disconnected.

If you're staring at the sea, they think you're brooding.

But if you've got a book open, you're safe. You don't have to explain yourself. You don't have to look available. You're invisible by choice.

And sometimes, invisibility is what you need to breathe properly.

I didn't read a single page.

But I left that café feeling like I'd heard something unspoken.

Not in words.

In glances. Silences. The rhythm of people trying to get through their afternoon without unravelling.

Back at the church, I sat.

Didn't light a candle.

Didn't pretend to pray.

Just sat there with an open book on my lap—still unread.

It didn't take long for me to drift again.

My creative mind was on fire.

Thérèse levitated silently and without resistance.

She looked amused, ready to process tons of miracles and magic tricks.

I was unconditional with myself.

Embracing my understanding of the Holy Spirit.

Ready to perform small miracles and magic tricks.

TWO EURO CANDLES

Chapter 63

For the Ones Who Never Came

Some people never come through the doors.

Not because they don't need to.

Because they don't know how. Or don't believe they're allowed. Or can't stand the idea of asking for something when no one's ever said yes.

I think about them often.

The friend who laughs at anything spiritual but can't sleep without the telly on because the silence gets too loud.

The girlfriend I dated once who called church "emotional theatre" but still kept her nan's rosary in the glovebox.

The kid who used to ride past on his bike and spit at the gates. Same time. Every day. Like clockwork. Like grief.

They never lit candles. Never sat in these pews. But I reckon they needed the flame more than most.

So today, I lit one for them.

Not because they'll ever see it.

But because sometimes love is lighting the candle for someone else's miracle—even if they never ask.

Thérèse didn't say anything. But I felt her smile.

"Do you think it still counts?" I asked aloud.

Of course it does.

That's the whole point of grace—it turns up for people even when they don't turn up for themselves.

The candle flickered, then steadied.

Outside, a bus rumbled past. A teenager glanced through the church doors, didn't come in, kept walking.

But the flame stayed lit.

And that was enough.

I light candles for my parents, siblings, wife, children and friends all the time.

They won't come in but are still able to receive, via proxy, some invisible protection.

Not many people are aware that Thérèse is mainly working remotely.

Accessible in places and locations unknown to the majority of us.

TWO EURO CANDLES

Chapter 64

Become The One Who Listens

It was small. Always was.

The wick was barely a thread. The wax had melted into something misshapen. Half the flame looked like it might give up any second.

But it didn't.

It burned.

It was my last day. The holy holiday had come to an end. The suitcases were locked and tagged.

I'd come in late that day. No phone. No words left. Just a want—to sit, to breathe, to see if the quiet would still make room for me.

And it did.

Someone had lit a candle hours earlier. I didn't know who. Could've been anyone. Could've been no one.

It had no name tied to it. No plea. No whisper. No folded note.

Just a flame, still going long after it should've given up.

I sat with it.

And as I watched it glow in the fading afternoon, I realised—I had changed.

I didn't need a sign anymore. I didn't need to hear Thérèse or feel some rush of wonder or clarity.

I just needed that light.

Not because it was spectacular. But because it stayed.

Through draughts. Through silence. Through disbelief.

It stayed.

And so did I.

Thérèse hadn't spoken for days. She'd warned me a few days ago. I didn't really believe her. I thought it was one of her tricks to keep me in charge. I was wrong. She was as quiet as a mouse.

Maybe she was done.

Maybe she was letting go.

Maybe she was watching from wherever the saints go when

their job is mostly done.

But just as I stood to leave, I heard her one last time.

Not loud. Not urgent.

Just kind.

"Now go. Become the one who listens."

I nodded.

And walked out.

Behind me, in the quiet of the holy silence,

the candle that stayed lit

burned on.

The station was ten minutes away.

I had plenty of time.

I returned the rental car the day before. My bag was packed. My boots were laced. The Airbnb key sat on the table with a thank-you note that I rewrote twice and still felt unsure about.

But I moved slowly.

Slower than needed.

Stopped halfway down the street to re-tie a perfectly tied shoelace.

Paused at a corner I'd passed a hundred times.

Stared into the window of the same café where I once ate the pancake too big for dignity.

And I knew what I was doing.

I was trying to miss the train.

Quietly. Subconsciously. Without blame.

Because leaving means facing everything I'd written.

Everything I hadn't.

It means deciding what to carry forward—what stays in the phone, what stays in me, what will be published, what the world will understand.

The platform was half-full when I arrived.

The train hadn't come yet.

Of course it hadn't.

I stood there, hands in pockets, and thought: What if I just… didn't?

What if I turned around?

Stayed another week?

Another hour?

What if I let this strange, gritty, rain-kissed city hold me a little longer?

But I knew.

Staying wouldn't hold the feeling.

Leaving wouldn't erase it.

The train arrived. Doors opened. People shuffled. I got on.

Found a seat by the window. Watched Ostend start to slide away in reverse.

The sea.

The church.

The pigeon who never came back.

I didn't cry.

I just whispered, "Thank you," like I was handing something back.

Not the city.

Myself.

That night, in Amsterdam airport, I lit no candle.

But I sat in stillness.

Breathed.

Opened the Google Docs one last time.

And wrote:

Thank you for having me.

To my surprise Thérèse gently answered me through the

power of my fingers and added:

Maxsense,

Since we met, you have always seemed like a kite high in the sky, anchored to the earth by a tiny string. Attached and detached at the same time. I am well aware that the view from above is much better—but it isn't meant for you. Today, there are divine invitations to wind yourself back to earth and enjoy a holy life. The world needs you—just as you are.

Thérèse

TWO EURO CANDLES

Acknowledgements

A big thank you to Maria and Frank.

About the author

Maxsense Maximus is a Belgian-born writer, born in Tongeren and raised in the Ardennes, whose formative environment cultivated a deep sensitivity to human behaviour, narrative nuance, and cultural subtext. In 1996, he migrated to Australia, where he encountered the complexities of cultural displacement—an experience that continues to inform the thematic architecture of his work.

His literary and psychological development was shaped by an acute perceptiveness from an early age: attuned to the moods, silences, and fractures of those around him, as well as to life events he experienced prematurely. A defining moment in his intellectual trajectory occurred during adolescence with the discovery of Ernest Hemingway's The Old Man and the Sea, which catalysed his interest in minimalist prose, internal conflict, and the intricacies of psychological realism.

Maximus's debut novel, Ostend, emerged from over two years of immersive observation and instinctive character construction. Composed largely in fragments during everyday life, the work reflects a creative process that prioritises authenticity over refinement, resulting in a narrative that is both emotionally resonant and formally raw. His writing style fuses cinematic detail with introspective depth, inviting the reader into a liminal space between memory, imagination, and emotional brilliance.

His latest book, Two Euro Candles, continues this exploration of lived and observed humanity. Set predominantly in Ostend, the novel is structured around his annual pilgrimage to the Church of Saint Peter and Saint Paul, where lighting €2 candles becomes both a literal and symbolic act of surrender, grief, and whispered prayer. Blending lyrical micro-narratives with irreverent theological dialogues with Saint Thérèse of Lisieux, Two Euro Candles interrogates the transactional nature of faith rituals while unearthing their potential for silent transformation. At its heart, the work is a meditation on trauma, exile, vulnerability, and the fragile beauty of authenticity in a world saturated with performance.

The pseudonym Maxsense Maximus is both an act of personal reclamation and symbolic transformation. Maxsense honours his mother's original wish to name him Maxence, while simultaneously articulating a literary philosophy that privileges perception as a pathway to creative and emotional abundance. Maximus, derived from Latin, situates his voice within a classical tradition of expressive depth and intentional precision. Maximus writes not to entertain, but to remember, to bear witness, and to engage with the emotional truths that often go unspoken.

TWO EURO CANDLES